TOPZ SECRET DIARIES

DANNY'S DARING DAYS

Alexa Tewkesbury

CWR

Copyright © CWR 2009

Published 2009 by CWR, Waverley Abbey House, Waverley Lane,
Farnham, Surrey GU9 8EP, UK. Registered Charity No. 294387.
Registered Limited Company No. 1990308. Reprinted 2010.

The right of Alexa Tewkesbury to be identified as the author of this
work has been asserted by her in accordance with the Copyright,
Designs and Patents Act 1988, sections 77 and 78.

See back of book for list of National Distributors.
Unless otherwise indicated, all Scripture references are from the
Good News Bible, copyright © American Bible Society 1966, 1971,
1976, 1992, 1994.
Concept development, editing, design and production by CWR
Illustrations: Helen Reason, Dan Donovan and CWR
Printed in Finland by Bookwell
ISBN: 978-1-85345-502-5

Hey, there! I'm Danny, a total sports nut, and I'm about to let you into my crazy, Topzy world! There's been tons of cool stuff going on lately with me and the Topz Gang. If you haven't met us before, just take a look over the page and you can read all about us.

Something I've been discovering is that God never gets fed up with showing us how to get closer to Him, no matter how many times we get in a muddle. He can even teach us through bad situations. In fact, sometimes, it's when things have gone <u>really</u> wrong that He can teach us the most! As long as we remember to keep talking to God, difficult times can definitely help us to learn lots of new things about Him and how to be His friend.

And speaking of friends, you've just got to get reading to find out how a brand-new friend showed me the way to move mountains – seriously! Better get page turning!

HI! WE'RE THE TOPZ GANG

– Topz because we all live at the 'top' of something …
either in houses at the top of the hill, at the top of the
flats by the park, even sleeping in a top bunk counts!
We are all Christians, and we go to Holly Hill School.

We love Jesus, and try to work out our faith in God
in everything we do – at home, at school and with our
friends. That even means trying to show God's love to
the Dixons Gang who tend to be bullies, and can be a
real pain!

If you'd like to know more about us, visit our website
at **www.cwr.org.uk/topz** You can read all about us,
and how you can get to know and understand the Bible
more by reading our 'Topz' notes, which are great fun,
and written every two months just for you!

PM

D'you know what, I'm sick of it! Sick, sick, sick, sick, SICK!! It is so totally, stupidly, mind-scramblingly, BRAIN-BOGGLINGLY UNFAIR!! And I mean that from the very back of my back teeth (which, by the way, are 'outstanding' the dentist told Mum at my check-up today). I wonder why Mum always does that – wait for the school holidays to get my teeth looked at. Well, let's face it, it's not the most fun day out you can ever have.

Although, there is one thing I'll say for our dentist: he is what he is. He doesn't pretend to be your friend one minute, then turn on you the next because you got picked for the Area Junior Football Squad and he didn't. Not that our dentist was very likely to get picked, I suppose. He's a bit old. To be a junior, that is. And bald. But that's not the point. You know exactly where you are with him. He always wears a white coat with a creepy little mask over his face so just his eyes show, and he tells you jokes while you're sitting in his chair with your mouth open. Then he has to remind you not to laugh, of course, because it might jog his rubbery glove hands while he's fishing around in your gums. (Not a problem, actually. His jokes don't tend to be funny. Except that one about the worm who went to get its teeth checked but the dentist couldn't find its mouth. That made me laugh.

Bit of a mistake. I had a mouthful of that pink rinsing stuff at the time. The nurse ended up with a pink-rinsing-stuff-patterned uniform, which some people might think looks interesting. Unfortunately, she wasn't one of them.)

Anyway, back to the point, of which there is a

MASSIVE

one. Benny is such an annoying great flat-footed noodle-head! And that's on a <u>good</u> day!

!!!

If the noodle-head ever starts speaking to me again, I'm going to tell him not to bother. I think I'll just stick with my dentist. You know where you are with someone who likes drilling teeth.

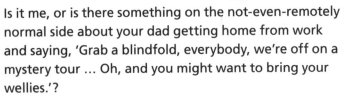

Is it me, or is there something on the not-even-remotely normal side about your dad getting home from work and saying, 'Grab a blindfold, everybody, we're off on a mystery tour … Oh, and you might want to bring your wellies.'?

I looked at Mum.

She said, 'I've just put the potatoes on.'

Dad said, 'What's a saucepan full of potatoes compared to the earth's rich bounty?'

I mean, majorly freaky, or what? Apart from anything

else, Dad's a real stickler for everything happening in the right order at the right time. Interrupting Mum's cooking now might mean supper not being on the table by seven o'clock on the dot as it usually is, which, according to Dad, could have a serious effect on his delicately-balanced body rhythms (whatever they are). Now, here he is breaking his own rules.

'What about supper?' Mum asked.

'For once,' announced Dad, 'I'm putting something far more exciting than supper on this evening's menu.'

'Fine,' said Mum. 'Danny, get your wellies.'

I suppose a lot depends on what you think of as exciting. Snow is exciting. It snowed last month. Me and the Gang, we built this massive snowman in the park and used a parsnip for its nose. Sarah said a parsnip would be better than a carrot because most people don't have orange noses, so why should a snowman put up with it. Benny pointed out that, as most people don't tend to have long, pointy vegetables for noses anyway, did it really matter, but Sarah said he was just being picky. In the end, because it stayed pretty cold for a while, our snowman was still there four days later – he just got smaller and a bit lopsided. We never found out what happened to the parsnip, though. It disappeared on day three. Josie said maybe a cat took it, but we all decided that wasn't very likely because cats don't eat parsnips – until Sarah said that her cat, Saucy, eats anything. Even her hair. Nice.

7

I tell you what else is exciting: being picked for the Area Junior Football Squad (which, by the way, you <u>weren't</u>, Benny). Christmas is exciting, too. And birthdays. Especially when you get exactly what you want without even having to ask for it, like I did last year with that ultra cool skateboard from Mum and Dad. I suppose I did have to drop a few hints … like about 173. But, who's counting? It's all worth it to see the expression on their faces when they know they've given you the absolute perfect present AND they think they've managed to come up with it all by themselves.

Anyway, back to the mystery tour. After Dad had driven Mum and me (in the back seat with our blindfolds on) to our secret destination (about five minutes away), he opened the door to let us out and said grandly, 'Now – take a look.'

We took our blindfolds off.

We looked.

'Um … what is it?' asked Mum.

'Well, we may not have our own garden, but this,' pronounced Dad, with a worryingly over-the-top hand gesture, 'is now our very own allotment.'

Mum shook her head slightly. She was obviously confused but trying incredibly hard not to be.

'Allotment?' she said.

'Yes, allotment,' repeated Dad proudly, gazing at a small patch of rough, lumpy, stinging nettle-infested dirt in front of us. 'From now on, this is where I'm going to grow all our own vegetables.'

'It's full of weeds,' Mum pointed out.

'Weeds?' Dad laughed. 'Weeds are all a part of the gardener's exciting challenge! I've been

8

reading a book. From now on, we can be do-it-yourself organic!'

'Good,' Mum replied, quite kindly I thought in the circumstances.

'Dad,' I said, 'do you have any understanding of the whole concept of "exciting"?'

***

John rang.

He said, 'What's up?'

I said, 'I could be wrong but I think my dad's just turned into an incredibly boring person.'

He said, 'I always thought your dad was pretty cool.'

'Me, too,' I said. 'Now he wants to do do-it-yourself gardening.'

'Right,' said John. 'Maybe that's just something that happens to all old people in the end.'

'Maybe,' I said.

'He might start spending time with Paul's dad. Paul's dad's into all that do-it-yourself sort of stuff.' said John.

'But is he a mad, vegetable-growing type of person?' I asked.

'Not sure,' answered John. 'I know he's got a shed.'

My room

Dad just poked his hands around my door and waved them at me madly.

'What do you see?' he asked.

'Your hands waving at me madly?' I suggested.

'No!' he said, as though I was going out of my way to miss the glaringly obvious. 'Green fingers!'

'Dad,' I said patiently, 'do you know anything about gardening?'

'Not a thing,' he shrugged, rubbing his green (not) fingers together. 'That's what makes it all so <u>exciting</u>.'

There's that word again. Sad, really. I'd almost go as far as to say bordering on the tragic.

'So,' he went on, 'how was the football training?'

'Good,' I said.

'Excellent,' he replied. 'Better get some sleep then. We're both going to be needing our energy. You for scoring goals, me for digging. No more lying about in bed on a Sunday morning for me. I shall be off down the road, working the land!'

Great. Dad's just found one more reason not to come to church with me.

WEDNESDAY 15

PM

Back from football training. Did loads of dribbling the ball practice, in and out of cones. Getting picked for the Area Junior Squad is actually pretty amazingly cool! Mr Richardson is a BRILLIANT coach. He told me today I'm a natural. He says my co-ordination works like a 'well-oiled trolley'. I rang John when I got home to tell him, but he just muttered in quite a frowny sort of way, 'To be honest, you don't see many trolleys playing football.'

Actually I think he's just jealous

because there's nothing oily or trolley-like about <u>him</u>.

And I <u>know</u> Benny's jealous. You should have seen his face when his name wasn't read out to be on the Squad after we'd done all those trials. He went off on a total rant first of all, but then he started making out that he was really pleased not to be picked, and that no one in their right mind would want to spend half the Easter holidays doing boring old football training just to be in some squiddly-diddly Squad. He said you've got all term to be told what to do and when to do it. Come the holidays, all he wanted was to be able to kick a ball <u>wherever</u> he liked <u>whenever</u> he liked. I reminded him that the 'wherever' he liked thing wasn't always such a good idea because last half-term he'd kicked a ball through Paul's mum's kitchen window, but he told me not to be such a pair of smarty pants.

Well, all I know is if you've got it, you've got it – and I guess Benny's just got to accept that he hasn't, so there's no point being all sour grapes and moody socks.

Been down the park showing Paul and Josie some of my 'well-oiled trolley' moves from training this morning. Josie wanted to have a go but Paul said it was OK, he'd just watch.

I said, 'You don't have to feel bad because you can't do it. There are lots of things <u>I</u> can't do, it's just that football isn't one of them.'

Paul said, 'I don't feel bad. I'm quite happy being a computer geek.'

'And let's face it,' Josie said helpfully, 'where would the world be without computer geeks?'

'Exactly,' Paul said. 'Probably with nothing on YouTube and seriously blogless.'

'Anyway,' I said, 'back to my stunning dribbling demonstration.'

That was when Dave and Benny turned up.

All I said was, 'Hey! You're just in time to watch my stunning demo of the art of dribbling,' and Benny went totally off on one again.

'Every time I see you, you're on about that stupid Area Squaddy stuff!' he yelled. 'Is that all you've got to do, keep showing off about how brilliant you are at football?'

I said, 'I'm not showing off. You just can't get over it because you didn't get picked. It's not my fault you're not good enough.'

Benny said, 'It's your fault you keep going on about it, though. Can't you talk about something else for five minutes?'

'Why should I?' I said. 'It's the first round next week and I really want our team to get through. We've got a good chance too. Mr Richardson says I'm a natural.'

'A natural what?' said Benny. 'Yoghurt?'

Then he stormed off.

'What is his problem?' I said to Paul.

'I'm not sure, but I think … maybe … <u>you</u> are,' he said.

'But what am I doing wrong? I'm good at football. Get over it.'

'I know you're good at football. We all know you're good at football. It's just …' He stopped.

'What?' I snapped.

He didn't answer.

'It's just …' Josie said quietly, 'well, sometimes you can sort of go on about it.'

Hang on a sec, he spoke to me! Down at the park, the noodle-head spoke to me. He said he was never going to speak to me again and he went and <u>spoke</u> to me. He can't even get <u>that</u> right.

Nipped into John's on my way back from the park. He was watching TV. Some arty programme about shaping a hedge into a double-decker bus. What's more, he was enjoying it. Quite alarming, really.

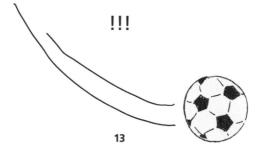

I said, 'John, have you ever heard me going on about how good I am at football?'

He said, 'Not sure. Maybe. A bit. Now and again. Do you want a crisp?'

!!!

What's the point of being in a gang if all they're going to do is wind you up and look down their noses? I am seriously not happy. Seriously, <u>seriously</u>. And even more than that.

***

Well, so what if I do tell people I'm good at football? It's only because I <u>am</u> good at football. There wouldn't be a lot of point in me going round saying, 'I'm really, really useless at football. Whatever happens, <u>don't</u> put me in the Area Squad.' At least I'm good at something. What's Benny good at, I'd like to know?

There's one thing about Dad. When he decides to get excited, he <u>really</u> gets excited. He just rang to say he'd be a bit late back from work because he was stopping off at the garden centre to buy essential equipment. Mum sighed and switched the cooker off.

'After all, Danny,' she said, 'what's a saucepan full of potatoes compared to the earth's rich bounty?'

I said, 'Mum, you know Dad tends to go on a bit when he gets really seriously into stuff?'

'Like organic gardening?' she suggested.

'Yes,' I said, 'like organic gardening. Well … am I like that?'

'About organic gardening?'

'No. About … say … football … for example.'

14

'Oh, yeah,' she said. 'Sometimes it's like living with a pair of demented owls.'

There are some questions you wish you'd never asked. Twit-twoo.

THURSDAY 16

AM

Been thinking about the demented owl thing. Maybe it's not so bad. I reckon I'd rather be called that than a show-off. Especially when I'm not showing off.

!!!

Just had five Weetabix for breakfast. Mr Richardson says we Squadders need to eat well so we have plenty of energy for training. (I was only going to have four but that left one on its own in the box which is just silly.)

***

Phone rang. Mum answered.

She said, 'Oh, hello. I'll get Danny.'

Then, 'It's that church youth leader,' she whispered, passing me the phone. She always calls Greg 'that church youth leader'. It's as if he doesn't have a name, or something.

I said, 'Hi, Greg. Sorry, I've got to go.'

He said, 'Where?'

I said, 'Area Junior Football Squad training.'

He said, 'I've just been hearing all about that.'

'Have you?' I said. 'Who from? Mr Richardson? Did he tell you I'm a natural?'

'It was Josie, actually,' he said. 'She's a bit upset.'

'Why?' I said. 'Don't tell me she doesn't want me to be in the Squad either.'

'No. She says you and Benny have had a really big fallout about it. Just wondered if I could help.'

'It's Benny's problem, not mine,' I said. 'I'm not the one causing trouble, he is.'

'Well,' Greg said, 'sometimes when things get in a muddle, it takes someone who's not involved to help sort it out. Do you want a chat later before band practice?'

'I'm not doing band practice this week,' I said. 'Maybe not for a few weeks till all the football's finished. Anyway, Benny's the one you should be talking to, not me. He's the one being stupid and jealous but he just won't see it. I've even prayed about it.'

'Have you? And what did you say?'

'What do you think?' I said. 'Dear Lord, please stop Benny being such an idiot.'

'Right,' said Greg. 'I'm not entirely sure that's a particularly helpful sort of prayer.'

I said, 'Sorry, Greg, but I'm going to have to go.'

'Of course,' he said. 'Just wanted you to know that I'm here if you need any help.'

Brilliant, now I'm late. Thanks, Josie. Thanks a lot.

Grrrrrr!

PM

I'm beginning to think that being in Topz is actually bottomz. Listen to this. Mr Richardson handed out our team shirts after training today. They are MEGA cool – green and white stripes with 'Area Junior Squad' across the back in black and a red star on the right shoulder! We are so going to be the team to end all teams. The rest of them don't stand a chance.

So anyway, I thought, I know what I'll do. I'll call in on Paul on my way home. I'll let him be the first to see my shirt.

I said, 'Paul, what do you think? Classic, or what?'

He said, 'Yeah, nifty. Have you made it up with Benny yet?'

I said, 'Why is everyone so interested in me and Benny? Don't you realise how important this match is next week? I'm not showing off, but if this tournament goes really well for me, I might even get spotted by some manager or something and end up turning pro.'

'Turning pro?'

'Yeah, you know,' I said. 'Professional.'

'OK,' said Paul.

OK? Is that it? I mean what does it take to get people excited round here?

'So,' said Paul, 'you'll have a few words with Benny then, right?'

Wrong. I've only got one word for Benny:

loser.

Next week when I'm the one who scores the goal that gets our team through to the next round, they are all going to be so sorry. I mean, all I want is a bit of support from my friends. Is that so much to ask?

'Dad,' I said, 'do you think I'm a show-off?'

'Hold that open a minute,' Dad said.

I stood there in the kitchen holding open a big bag of plant-growing compost while he scooped some out with his hands and dropped it into six yoghurt pots – at least the idea was that it went into the yoghurt pots, but most of it ended up on the floor.

'Sorry,' he said when he'd finished, 'what was the question?'

'It doesn't matter.'

!!!

Dad's not very good at listening. I mean, he can be really supportive sometimes. He was brilliant helping me out with all my training for the fun run last summer. I don't think I'd ever have won that trophy if it hadn't been for him. And he taught me everything he knows about table tennis – which admittedly isn't a lot but, hey, never look up a gift horse's nose or you might find two in the bush … or however it goes. In fact, Dad's normally pretty interested in all my sport. It's just that listening's not a big thing with him. Especially when he's in a craze phase, like now. Mum says that when he gets stuck into a brand-new project, that's all he can think about, so it's not even worth trying to have a conversation. Unless it's about the new project, of course.

They're great, though, Mum and Dad, they really are. I just wish they knew God like I do. If they did, I don't suppose Greg would be just 'that church youth leader' to Mum. And Dad might be pleased I sometimes play my trumpet in the worship band on a Sunday morning, instead of wondering why I don't join a 'proper' group. And they both might be happy for me. Happy that I've made friends with God instead of waiting for me to grow out of it.

I wish I could talk to them about God. Not all the time, just now and again. Paul talks about Him to his mum and dad. So does Dave. And John and Sarah and Josie. Even Benny. It's just me. It's always just me.

Sometimes I feel all on my own.

***

I suppose I could ask Mum what to do about Benny but she'll probably just say I'm being a wombat. That's what she usually calls me when I start on about someone. 'If you're big enough to eat five Weetabix for breakfast, you're big enough to sort out your tiffs by yourself. Stop being a wombat.'

I'm not, though. Being a wombat. It's Benny. He needs to get over himself. I'm in the Squad and he's not. Big deal. If he can't cope with it, I don't see how we're going to be able to stay friends. Football's what I do. It's who I am. I'm not going to start playing like a baked bean just to please him.

FRIDAY 17

AM

Dad's taken over the kitchen windowsill with yoghurt pots full of compost. Well, eleven yoghurt pots and a coleslaw tub.

Mum said, 'What's all this dirt doing in my kitchen?'

Dad said, 'Don't touch those pots! There's a runner bean seed in each one. Before you know it, it'll be like "Jack and the Beanstalk" in this flat.'

Mum raised her eyebrows. 'Don't tell me you're trying to breed hens that lay golden eggs?'

Dad said, 'Well, now you're just being silly.'

'Fine,' Mum answered. 'They can stay where they are as long as nothing starts creeping around. But I'm warning you, the first whiff of greenfly and they're out.'

PM

Sarah and John have gone away for the weekend. Paul's trying to explain to his dad what a blog is (although why his dad wants to know is beyond me. Blogs are for people with interesting stuff to write about and not people like Paul's dad who, according to Paul, gets hysterically happy when something like a door falls off because that means he can rush around fixing it.). Dave's gone to a tent exhibition with his mad-about-camping-used-to-be-a-boy-scout uncle, and Josie's gone shopping with her mum. Isn't that just so typical? Here I am, dying to go down the park for a kick about so I can practise some of that stuff we did at training this morning, and the only person around is Benny. Like <u>he's</u> really going to want to come with me.

Mum said, 'What have you got to look so fed up about?'

'I wanna play football,' I said.

She said, 'I thought you were playing football all morning.'

I shrugged. Sometimes there's no point going on about it. Mum will never understand the 'I was born to play football' thing.

She said, 'Why don't you pop down to the park on your own?'

'Because that would just look sad,' I pointed out.

'I don't see why,' she said. 'It'd be better than having you moping around here. You're making me feel like a damp Wednesday.'

'Thanks.'

'Well, all I can say is you can think yourself lucky your father's not home yet. He'd have you down that

21

allotment digging out nettles before you can say Jack and the yoghurt pots.'

Good point. For safety's sake, I think I might grab a ball and go and look sad down by the goal posts.

My room

The trouble with looking sad down by the goal posts is that you end up <u>feeling</u> sad. The Dixons Gang sloped by, fortunately just at the moment when I'd shot the ball slap-bang dead centre through the goal – yesss! Unfortunately they were still there when I followed this by punching the air and performing a victory cartwheel that went slightly adrift so I ended up sitting on my bottom in a mud patch.

'Aww!' they said. 'Hasn't little Danny-poos got any of his Topzy-wopzy friends to play with today? Poor diddums muddy pants.'

It's one thing being called names by Dixons when I'm out with the Gang. It's another thing altogether when I'm out on my own. This is all Benny's fault.

Maybe I should just take the bull by the horns (or the sheep by the hair curlers as Dad insists on saying) and go and see Benny right now. After all, we used to be friends. We ought to be able to talk about stuff like this. Besides, Dad'll be home soon. If I don't go out he'll be coming into my bedroom with a trowel for me as a special treat.

Back in my room

Went and stood outside Benny's front door. I'd thought about what I was going to say. I'd got it all sorted out in my head. I'd even practised how I was going to say it. Then I was ready to face him.

Before I got round to ringing the bell, Benny's dad got home from work.

'Hello, Danny,' he said. 'You looking for Benny?'

'Er, no, not really,' I said. 'Why?'

He said, 'Possibly because you're standing outside our flat?'

'Ah,' I said.

'Would you like me to go and get him?' he asked.

'No,' I said. 'I was only … doing some … indoor fitness training. This just seemed like a good place to stop and have a bit of a … stretch.'

'Right,' said Benny's dad. 'Good.'

I think I got away with it.

This is all so stupid! And annoying. And pathetic. And pointless. And unbelievably BORING. Yes, I am now actually bored with arguing with Benny.

***

I wonder if Benny's bored arguing with me? Probably not. He's too much of a noodle-head.

Rang Greg.

I said, 'You know you said you'd always help me?'

23

'Of course,' he said.

I said, 'Well, could I have some help at youth club, please? And could Benny have some too because he's honestly being a complete noodle-head?'

'Absolutely,' Greg said. 'See you there.'

Never again. Never, ever, EVER again. Youth club's just a big poo.

SATURDAY 18

AM

In bed. Probably going to stay here for the rest of my life. Or at least until the first round Squad match next week.

Had my 'helpful' chat with Greg and Benny. It went like this:

Greg: So, what's all this about a fallout?

Benny: What's all what about a fallout?

Greg: It's not like you two to quarrel. What's the problem?

Benny: Danny. He's the problem.

Me: That is so not fair. Can I help it if I'm better at football than you?

Benny: You're not better at football than me. You were just lucky.

Me: I'm better at football than anybody in school.

Benny: No. You're just the biggest show-off of anybody in school.

Greg: Hang on –

Me: How many times? I am <u>not</u> showing off!

Benny: You SO are.

Me: Well, you're just jealous.

Benny: So? I'd rather be jealous than a show-off.

Greg: Now let's –

Me: Well, I'd rather be a show-off than useless at football.

Benny: I AM NOT USELESS AT FOOTBALL!

Greg: RIGHT, THAT'S ENOUGH!

SILENCE

Greg: Arguing never solved anything. One of you got picked for the Squad. One of you didn't. It really doesn't matter that much, and it's certainly not worth all this. God loves both of you and He's given you both amazing talents, whether they're to do with being good at football or being the world's fastest … speed-knitter! If you want to shout about something, shout about that. Shout about how special you are to Him. Shout about what a fantastic plan He's got for your life. Instead of harping on about who's best at what, ask Him to show you how you can use the gifts He's given you for Him. Thank Him for who you are and what you can do. And stop being angry with each other. OK?

Like I say, youth club's just a big poo.

***

I wonder if there is such a thing as a world's fastest speed-knitter.

Mum knocked on my door.

'Are you planning on getting up today or shall I give your breakfast to the bean seeds?'

'Give it to who you like,' I said.

'Don't you want to see them?' she said.

'Who?' I asked. 'The bean seeds?'

'No!' she said. 'The new people moving into the ground-floor flat. Right now. As we speak.'

'Not really,' I said.

'Don't you care that we're getting new neighbours?'

'Well, they're not exactly "neighbours", are they?' I grunted. 'I mean, from where we are, they're a long way down.'

!!!

Lord God, what's happened to Greg? I'm facing a massive test of my footballing brilliance next week and even he's turning against me. Maybe this is what it's like if you're super-talented. You become an outcast because other people can't stand not being as good as you are.

And what did he mean about talents coming from You? I know You give me lots of good stuff, like food, for example, but as far as football's concerned Mr Richardson says I'm a natural. That means it's naturally in me, doesn't it? And sorry, but if it's naturally in me, what's that got to do with You?

PM

Finally got up. Big mistake. Dad pounced on me.

'Danny! How about you and me scoot off to the allotment and make something grow?'

'Dad,' I said, 'how about not?'

'Come on, where's your sense of adventure?' he said. 'Besides, what else are you going to do?'

'I don't know,' I said, 'but if I sit here for long enough, I'm sure I'll think of something.'

'Sorry, but I'm not taking no for an answer,' he insisted. 'Off we go.'

The thing about parents is they should come with some kind of warning device that flashes or bleeps, or both, to let you know in plenty of time when to keep your head down and pretend you've got to learn the entire Oxford English Dictionary by heart for a test. In fact, in extreme cases of parental interference, I think it should be compulsory. And let's face it, it doesn't get more extreme than being forced to do gardening.

I looked at Mum, hoping she'd be able to come up with a cunning escape plan for me. She tried her best.

'It'll be months before you'll get anything to grow in that wasteland,' she said. 'You can't see the earth for the weeds.'

'Nonsense,' retorted Dad. 'It's nothing a spade won't sort out.'

'A spade?' scoffed Mum. 'More like a JCB.'

'You know your trouble?' Dad said. 'You have no imagination. Danny. Wellies.'

Warning lights. It's the only solution. Enormous, red, beaming, flashing warning lights. With bleepers. And sirens. And everything.

Allotment excavations cut short. Dad attacked a huge clump of stinging nettles and broke his spade.

Dave rang.

He said, 'I tried you earlier but your mum said you were out.'

'Oh,' I said.

'Where have you been?' he asked.

'Please don't ask,' I answered.

'Why not?' he said.

'Because that would mean I'd have to tell you and I can't cope with the embarrassment.'

'Right,' he said. 'Do you want to come to a barbeque?'

'When?' I asked.

'This evening. It's my uncle's idea. He says food should always be cooked in the open air and eaten round a campfire. I did point out that we couldn't really have a campfire in the garden but he said a barbeque's the next best thing. So, anyway, are you coming?'

'Sounds good,' I said. 'Who else is going?'

'Well, there's my uncle, Mum and Dad, me.'

'Any Topz?'

'Oh, yeah,' he said, 'you can't have a barbeque without Topz.'

'Which ones?' I asked.

'Well, John and Sarah are away.'

'I know,' I said, 'so which ones?'

'Oh, you know, Paul, Josie, you. All the usual.'

'All the usual as in Benny.'

'Well, yeah, possibly. I mean, probably. I mean, I asked him and he sort of said …'

'What?'

'Well … yes.'

***

To be honest, I'm not really in the mood for a barbeque. Dave says they're all going down the park first to play footie. Apparently his uncle's a pretty mean goalkeeper on top of knowing all about being a boy scout. At least, that's what his uncle says. To be honest, I'm not really in the mood for playing footie either. The match next week is too important and I've been training every day. I don't want to overdo it or I might get stale. Dave says it's daft not to go just because of a silly argument with Benny. He says I can't avoid him forever.

I said, 'It's got nothing to do with having an argument with Benny. I'm just not really in the mood.'

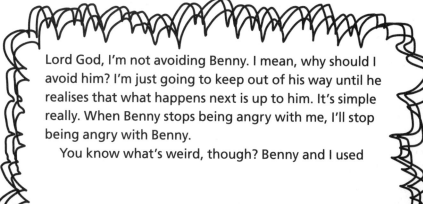

Lord God, I'm not avoiding Benny. I mean, why should I avoid him? I'm just going to keep out of his way until he realises that what happens next is up to him. It's simple really. When Benny stops being angry with me, I'll stop being angry with Benny.

You know what's weird, though? Benny and I used

to pray together. He's prayed with me about Mum and Dad coming to church. Now I'm not even in the mood for going to a barbeque with him. Loopy or what?

Josie rang. (Mum says she's thinking of having the phone moved into my room because all the calls are for me. Cool.)

Before Josie could say anything annoying like, 'Why aren't you coming to the barbeque?', I said, 'If this is about the barbeque, I'm just not in the mood.'

'No,' she said, 'it's about worship band at church in the morning. Apparently Tom can't play because he's ill so I said I'd ask you if you'd do it instead.'

'Oh,' I said.

'So, will you?' she said.

'I can't,' I said. 'I haven't done any practice. I've been too busy with Squad.'

Josie said, 'But I'll be there, I'm violining, and it's all stuff you've played before.'

'I would if I could,' I said, 'but I really can't. I've got to concentrate on the first round next week.'

'But we need you, Danny,' she insisted. 'It's not the same without some trumpet.'

'Well, I'm sorry and everything, but the Squad needs me too.'

Josie said, 'Don't you think you're taking all this Squad stuff a bit too seriously?'

'No,' I snapped. 'Don't you think you're taking worship band a bit too seriously?'

'No, actually,' she answered. 'I'm playing in worship band for God. Who are you playing football for?'

I hate it when people do that – make you feel guilty for doing absolutely nothing in this whole, enormous, massive, wide world wrong. What's the matter with everyone? I'll play in worship band again when we've won the football. Mr Richardson says the most important thing to do now is focus. That means saving my energy; putting everything I've got into the Squad. If I blow my lungs out playing trumpet, how's that going to help? I mean, it's only a few weeks of missing worship band. Talk about making a big deal out of a squished biscuit. What is the problem here?

In bed

Dad's been trying to mend his spade whilst rambling on about root vegetables. If Josie wants to see someone who really <u>is</u> too serious about something, she should come and sit here with him. Still, on the plus side, he does seem very happy. Which is more than I can say for me.

***

Lord God, You know how important the Squad is to me, don't You? It's more important than anything. It could have a really massive effect on what I'm going to do for the rest of my future life in the future of futures, ie be a professional footballer. Worship band's cool but football's what I'm a natural at. I'll get back to band practice once we've won the tournament, promise, I just can't let the team down now. Why doesn't anyone understand?

SUNDAY 19

PM
Went to church.
Didn't really feel
like it (well, why
would I when all
everyone wants to do
is make me feel bad
about being good at football?), but went anyway.

After Sunday Club, Greg said, 'When's the big match, then?'

'Tuesday,' I said.

'Are you looking forward to it?' he asked.

'You bet I am,' I said. 'Although I'd be looking forward to it more if my friends hadn't all turned against me.'

'They haven't turned against you,' Greg smiled.

'They so have,' I argued. 'Benny thinks all I am is a show-off and Josie wants me to spend my life blowing a trumpet.'

Greg said, 'Sit down a minute.'

Oh, here it comes. The chat. The 'I really do understand how you're feeling' talk, even though it's as plain as a ready-salted crisp that, actually, no, you don't.

'Did you understand what I was trying to say after youth club on Friday?' Greg asked.

'You mean when you were telling me off?'

'I wasn't telling you off, I was trying to make myself heard,' he grinned. 'And, believe me, that was no mean feat given the racket you and Benny were making.'

That's fair, I suppose. We were definitely hammer and tonging it.

Then, Greg suddenly flipped open his Bible. He can do that, I've noticed. He never seems to have to hunt for anything. He just does this kind of super-quick flippy, flicky thing and, hey pesto pasta, there he is on exactly the right page, looking at exactly the right verse which just happens to say exactly the right thing to help him explain what he's getting at – exactly. In fact, I reckon Greg could be a world record holder in Bible-flipping and verse-finding. After all, if there can be world's fastest speed-knitters, why not world's fastest Bible-flippers?

'Read that,' Greg said.

He was pointing to a bit in 1 Peter, chapter 4:

'Each one, as a good manager of God's different gifts, must use for the good of others the special gift he has received from God. Whoever preaches must preach God's messages; whoever serves must serve with the strength that God gives, so that in all things praise may be given to God through Jesus Christ ...'

I zipped once through it quickly. Then I read it again more slowly.

I asked (a bit quietly in case I'd completely missed the point and ended up sounding less like a questioning sort of person and more like a banana-brain), 'Are you saying this applies to football?'

'Pardon?' Greg said.

(Louder) 'Are you saying this applies to football?'

'It applies to anything,' Greg answered.

Phew. At least I'd escaped the banana-brain thing. Next question.

'How, though?'

Well, I had to ask. To be honest, it is quite hard to see how playing football can have anything to do with what it says in the Bible.

'Because God is our Father in heaven,' Greg said. 'Every amazing thing we are is because of Him. Every brilliant talent we have is a gift from Him. And I'm not just talking about being gifted at sport or music or painting. Gifts from God come in all shapes and sizes. People can be sensationally gifted at caring for others, for instance; or at talking to people; or at organising special events; even at serving others – collecting up song books on a Sunday morning to tidy up the church, or making visitors a cup of coffee  to help them feel welcome. Those are all gifts, talents, things different people are good at. And everything we're good at we can use for God.'

'But,' I said, 'how can I use football for God? I mean, it's football, isn't it? It's not about being kind or helpful or making people feel welcome. It's football.'

'And football's something you're really good at,' answered Greg, 'which is fantastic, especially for your team. But what you have to try and remember when people are slapping you on the back and saying, "Wow, Danny, that was a goal in a million!" is that all that ability comes from God. It's naturally in you, yes, but that's because God put it there. So don't take it for granted and try not to show off about it. Instead, thank God for giving you that talent, then enjoy it and get stuck into it for all you're worth. And while you're doing that, ask Him how you can use your gift for Him.

Ask Him how you can make a difference with the skills He's given you. Maybe you could say to someone who doesn't know Him yet, "Yes, that was a goal in a million, but actually it's all thanks to God."'

My bedroom

Greg's OK actually. After Friday, I was worried he might be losing it. I was thinking, oh no, if I can't talk to Greg, who on earth else am I going to talk to? I mean, all Dad wants to talk about lately is turnips.

But, it's all right, Greg's still cool. He still knows you need sorting out even before you realise it yourself. And he can still come up with just the right thing to say to hit the nail of the matter smack on its knobbly little head. In fact, Greg could probably drink a cup of coffee, eat a Mars bar and recite the alphabet backwards, all at the same time. I reckon that must be his gift. Not the Mars bar backwards alphabet bit, obviously. But talking to people. Understanding how they feel. Flipping to the bits in the Bible that explain everything you need to know in an egg cup ... or is that a nutshell ...? Or possibly even an eggshell ...

Dear Lord, I think I'm beginning to get it. Me being good at football isn't actually about me at all. It's about You and what You've given me to make me into the person I am – to make me into Danny. I'm sorry if I've been showing off. I haven't meant to. It's just hard when you can see that you're good at something and someone else isn't. It kind of makes you a bit ... well ... showy-offy.

I know I'm good at football and I really like it that I am. But now, when I'm playing, I'm going to try not to think about me. I'm going to try to play for You. I'll work as hard as I can at it and do my best to find a way to let people know that the only reason I'm any good at anything is because of You. And every time I score a goal, I'm not going to leap around madly thinking, oh aren't I clever. I'm going to say thank you to <u>You</u>.

Had a weird thought. I know I don't quite get it when Dad gets all crazy-phasey about stuff like organic gardening, but I suppose I've got to admit that when he does get excited about something, he really does get … well … excited. So, I was imagining what he might be like if he started coming to church with me and got to talk to Greg and to find out about God. I mean, if Dad actually gave his life to God, he'd be the most excited Christian on the planet, I reckon!

And then I started thinking, but actually we should all be the most excited Christians on the planet because God's given us so much to be excited about. For a start I'm in the tournament next week. I'm actually in the Squad! And I've got the green and white striped shirt to prove it. Thank You, God.

Which brings me to my next thought … Benny.

Noodle head

✳ I could ring him up.

✳ On the other hand, I could go round and see him.

✳ But what if he still doesn't want to talk to me?

✳ Advantages of ringing him up (assuming he still hates me):

> He won't have to talk to me if he doesn't want to because if someone else picks up the phone, he can do lots of hand gesturing to let the phone answerer know that he doesn't want to speak to me. If <u>he</u> picks up the phone he can pretend he can't hear anything and just put it down again when he realises who it is.

✳ Advantages of going round to see him (assuming he still hates me):

> He'll have to talk to me whether he wants to or not because either he'll answer the door himself or, when his mum or dad answer the door, they'll be bound to invite me in to see him – in which case no amount of hand gesturing will help because I'll know he's at home. In other words, no advantages at all.

<u>That's settled then – I'll ring him up.</u>
Now.
No time like the present.
Strike while the iron's in the oven.
I mean, why put off till tomorrow
what you can argue about today?

On the other hand, maybe I'll just give it half an hour.

37

It's amazing how quickly time whips by when you're trying to put off doing something you really don't want to do, and you end up letting your dad witter on endlessly about the advantages of being able to pickle his own cabbage.

One hour later

'Dad,' I said. 'Please can I use the phone?'

'Go ahead,' he said.

'Are you sure? I mean, there isn't someone you want to ring up? Incredibly urgently? Like now, for instance?'

'Nope,' he replied. 'I'm going to inspect my beans.'

This is it, then. The moment of the phone call. Now or never. Never or now even. Here goes:

Benny: Hello?

Me: Benny?

Benny: Yup.

Me: Danny.

Benny: Yup.

Me: Had a chat with Greg.

Benny: Me, too.

Me: Really?

Benny: He told me not to be jealous.

Me: Wow. He told me not to be a show-off.

Benny: Wow. He told me that God's given everyone different gifts and just because one person is better at something than someone else, that doesn't make them any more special, because we're all equal in our specialness. Not that you are, of course.

Me: What, equal in my specialness?

Benny: No. Better at football than me.

Me: Oh, yeah, of course. Besides, Greg told me that all the gifts we have come from God, so we should remember to thank Him for them and try to find ways to use them for Him.

Benny: Did he say how that applies to football?

Me: Sort of. Anyway, I'm working on it, but what I really wanted to say was, sorry I've been a show-off.

Benny: Yeah, well, sorry I've been jealous.

Me: No probs.

SLIGHTLY AWKWARD PAUSEY MOMENT.

Benny: Do you fancy having a kickabout down the park?

Me: Well … yeah. When?

Benny: Five minutes?

Me: Stonking.

Benny: Triffic.

ANOTHER PAUSEY MOMENT BUT NOT QUITE AS AWKWARD AS THE FIRST ONE.

Me: So, Benny, we're OK then, yeah?

Benny: Well, I've always been OK. Not so sure about you, though.

Cool. Double cool. Triple, even. With squirty cream and marshmallows. I suppose sometimes it takes a really big argument to make you realise how pointless it is doing really big arguing.

MONDAY 20

AM

Bad news – back to school. Summer term starts today. Good news – just done early morning fitness training with Benny.

Benny said, 'Is there anything I can help you with for the first-round match tomorrow?'

I said, 'We've only got one more Squad practice but I was going to do some fitness training before school. D'you want to come?'

'Try and stop me,' Benny said. (I've missed Benny. This not arguing thing is just so mega.)

So anyway, there we were before school, doing laps round the park, sit-ups, press-ups, squat thrusts and star jumps. Impressively impressive, if I say so myself.

I said to Benny, 'Don't you just love keeping fit?'

He grunted, 'Yeah ... groovy ... can we stop now? Need food.'

That's the quite comforting thing about Benny. Whatever you're doing, wherever you're doing it, you can always rely on one thing: he never stops being hungry.

PM

Squad training after school was ace-in-your-face. I scored THREE goals!

When I went to get changed, Mr Richardson grinned at me and said, 'Keep oiling that trolley!'

In bed

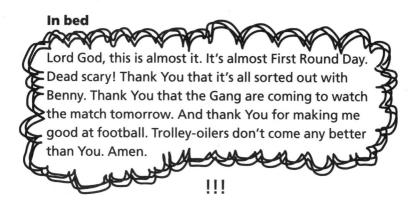

Lord God, this is almost it. It's almost First Round Day. Dead scary! Thank You that it's all sorted out with Benny. Thank You that the Gang are coming to watch the match tomorrow. And thank You for making me good at football. Trolley-oilers don't come any better than You. Amen.

!!!

Talk about the unexpected happening unexpectedly.

Dad poked his head round my door and said, 'What time's the match tomorrow?'

I said, 'Four o'clock.'

He said, 'See you there.'

I said, 'Really? I thought you'd forgotten.'

He said, 'Forgotten? How could I forget Area Junior Squad First Round Day?'

'Well,' I said, 'you have been a bit preoccupied with … beans.'

'Nonsense,' he said. 'I can grow a few beans and still remember to turn up for a football match. It's called multitasking.'

PM

I can't believe it. I just can't believe it. It's over. And I just can't believe it …

Why, Lord? Why did You go away? More to the point, why did You take my gift away? I mean, if You were going to take it away like that, why did You have to wait until match day? Why did You even have to give it to me in the first place?

Paul rang.

He said, 'It's all right, you know. Even the most brilliant people have times when their brilliance can go a bit … sort of … manky.'

manky

Benny rang.

He said, 'It's all right, you know. Nobody can be brilliant all the time. Not even brilliantly brilliant people like you and me.'

not brilliant

Josie rang.

She said, 'It's all right, you know. Just because you weren't brilliant today doesn't mean you're not still brilliant.'

not still brilliant

Dave rang.

He said, 'It's all right, you know –'

'It's <u>not</u> all right!' I shouted. 'It is <u>so</u>

it's all right

NOT ALL RIGHT!'

In bed

Someone came into my room.

I couldn't see who it was because
I had my duvet over my head, but I 'sensed' it was
Mum. Of course, it helped when she started speaking.

Mum said, 'You don't have to hide away just because
you missed a goal.'

I didn't answer.

'Your dad and I have been talking,' she said, 'and,
really, that ball could so easily have gone in.'

I still didn't answer.

Mum said, 'I thought you looked just like a proper
footballer in all your stripy gear. Quite a superstar,
really.'

Mouth zipped.

'You know, Danny,' Mum sighed, 'you could be really
grown-up about all this and think, oh well, missing a
goal can happen to anyone. Better luck next time.'

Nope. Not speaking.

'Or you could behave like a complete wombat and
spend the rest of your life under that duvet.'

Welcome to the wombat zone.

'Fine,' said Mum. 'Wombats it is.'

Then she went.

I shouldn't ignore her. It's not <u>her</u> fault. I know
it's not her fault. It's just I've got nothing to say, and
sometimes –

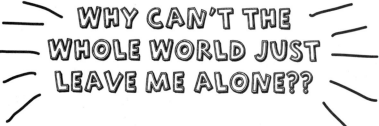

WHY CAN'T THE
WHOLE WORLD JUST
LEAVE ME ALONE??

WEDNESDAY 22

AM

Twelve laps round the park.
Forty star jumps.
Twenty press-ups.
Twenty sit-ups.
YAAAAYY!

Forget it. I am SO not doing any of that. Ever again. I think I'm going to take up bean watching. Well, why not? It works for Dad.

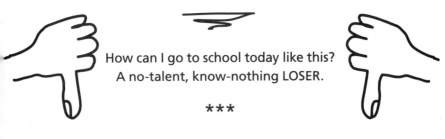

How can I go to school today like this?
A no-talent, know-nothing LOSER.

***

I said to Dad, 'Dad, can I not go to school today, please?'

He said, 'Why don't you want to go to school?'

I said, 'Why d'you think? The one thing I'm any good at, apparently I'm not any good at.'

He said, 'You're good at lots of things. Don't be so defeatist. Anyway, one broken egg doesn't ruin the whole box. Chances are it'll go much better next time.'

I said, 'But that's the whole point. There isn't going to be a next time. We're out of the tournament.'

'Out of <u>this</u> tournament, maybe. But there'll be plenty of others.'

'No, there won't,' I said. 'I'm useless. I'm never playing football again. So, anyway, can I?'

'Can you what?'

'Stay at home today.'

'Absolutely not,' Dad said.

'Oh, pleeeeaase!' I said pleeeeaadingly. 'I'll dig out every weed in the allotment.'

'Really?' Dad said.

'Definitely,' I nodded.

'Absolutely not.'

I said to Mum, 'Mum, can I not go to school today, please?'

She said, 'Why? Don't you feel well?'

I said, 'Yes … well, no … well, what I feel is … useless.'

She said, 'What, just because you missed a goal?'

I said, 'There's nothing "just" about it.'

She said, 'You'd better get a move on. The next thing you'll miss is the bus.'

'I don't care,' I mumbled.

'You'll have a long walk, then,' she answered.

'Fine,' I snapped.

'Wombat,' she muttered.

'Parent,' I grunted.

I don't want anyone to look at me.

I don't want anyone to talk to me.

I need something to make me invisible.

!!!

I can't even pray.

This is the worst day of my life. (Apart from yesterday.)

PM

Been thinking more seriously about the whole 'How can I make myself invisible?' thing. It's the only answer. I wonder if Paul could invent something. He's good at stuff like that. He makes things out of almost nothing. He once made his mum some perfume for her birthday out of crushed rose petals and Ribena. It wasn't great. It made purple stains on her neck and when Paul's dad came home he said, 'What's that awful smell?' But the point is, he had a go, so he could have a go at making me invisible. Even if he could only make half of me invisible it would help. Especially if it was the top half. I mean, let's face it, there aren't many people who are going to bother talking about football to a pair of legs walking around on their own. I could go to school, do all my maths and stuff that Mum and Dad keep telling me is so important, without having to say anything to anyone.

Unlike today.

Today I had to talk to everyone. Everyone who saw the match. Anyone who was on the Squad.

They said things like, 'Hey, Danno, what happened to you yesterday?'

And, 'It's not like you to let the side down.'

And, 'Can't believe you missed that goal. It was a cinch.'

I need to be invisible.

46

Vanishing Man.
Mr Nobody.

My room

Door bell went.

I yelled out to Mum, 'If it's for me, I'm not here.'
Next minute, Benny and Josie walked in.

Thanks, Mum. Since when did 'I'm not
here' mean 'Oh, yes, please invite the whole
world into my bedroom'?

'We just came round to say sorry,' said
Josie.

'Why, what have you done?' I answered.
'It's not what <u>we've</u> done, it's more ...' She
stopped.

'More what <u>I've</u> done, you mean,' I finished
for her. 'Like losing the Area Junior Football
Squad tournament. Yeah, thanks for pointing that out.'

'That's not fair,' said Benny. 'We're sorry it went
wrong for you, that's what Josie means.'

'Well, don't be,' I muttered. 'I don't want anyone
feeling sorry for me. Especially not you.'

'Anyway,' said Josie, 'we just wondered if you wanted
to go down the park. We thought you could show us
some more stuff you learnt at Squad training.'

'Don't you get it?' I said. 'I'm not doing that any
more. I didn't learn anything. I lost the match.'

'That's rubbish,' said Benny. 'You were part of a
whole team. The whole team lost, it wasn't just you.'

I said, 'Try telling that to the rest of the Squad. More
to the point, try telling that to Mr Richardson. Didn't
you see his face yesterday? It had "Fantastic. What a
brilliant time for the wheels to come off your trolley!"

written all over it. Anyway, why do you care so much? You never wanted me to be in the Squad in the first place.'

'I thought we'd sorted all that out,' Benny replied. I suppose he did look a bit upset, but that's not my problem. He should feel the way I'm feeling.

'All right, so you don't want to play football,' Josie said, 'but I'm going down to band practice later. We could go together.'

'Why?' I grumbled. 'Worship band is about doing something for God. Isn't that what you said? What's the point? I mean what's He ever done for me?'

That's when I saw Josie glance at Benny. Benny nodded.

'What?' I snapped.

'It's just …' Josie began. 'The thing is … You see, we were wondering … I mean, only if you were happy with it and everything …'

'What she's trying to say is,' interrupted Benny, 'would you like us to pray with you?'

'What?'

'Because,' Josie said, 'when things haven't gone how you wanted and you're just sort of dying inside with disappointment, God can really help. Like when I was going to get a kitten and I'd been and chosen one and everything. And then Dad decided we just really didn't live in the right sort of place to have one, so it never happened, and I was so disappointed and I went round to Sarah's and cried all afternoon and – '

'No!' I shouted.

'No what?' Josie said.

'No, I don't want you to pray with me! How is God

48

going to help me now? He should have helped me yesterday. That's when I needed Him. That's when He should have been there. But what did He do? He went away and left me to lose the match. And speaking of going away,' I added, 'that's what I'd like you to do. Now, please.'

It must have sounded horrible. But that's how I feel. Horribly horrible.

In any case, how can I be Vanishing Man if people insist on being able to see me?

In bed

Mum came in. It's astonishing how un-private your own bedroom can be. She was holding an envelope.

'Who in the world would be delivering cards at this time of night, I have no idea,' she said, 'but someone just poked this under the door for you.'

I waited for Mum to go. She obviously wasn't going to. When it comes to privacy, parents have so much to learn.

I opened the envelope. Inside was a card with a picture of a huge great polar bear lying on its back in the snow, and wrapped up in its paws was a tiny polar bear cub.

There was a message in the card written in green ink:

To Danny
'God has always been your defence; his eternal arms are your support.'
Deuteronomy 33:27
God loves you THIS much.
FRom GReg

'Well?' Mum asked. 'Who's it from?'
'No one.'

THURSDAY 23

AM

Can't sleep. Don't think I've slept all night. I still feel horrible. Inside, outside, all over. And it's barely even light yet.

***

If God's eternal arms are supposed to be supporting me, where did He put them on Tuesday?

PM

We read a poem in Literacy this morning. Not sure what it was all about except that there was a mountain and a shivering stream in it. When we'd finished, Mr Mallory said that as it was so warm today, packed lunch people could eat outside. Well, what he actually said was, 'Those of you who've brought your own sustenance may spread yourselves under the sky and soak in some rays from this glorious burst of spring sunshine.' Basically he meant sarnies on the grass.

I actually think Mr Mallory could be a poet. Not that anyone would probably understand a word he wrote. It's hard enough understanding a word he <u>says</u> half the time, but it can be a bit like that with poets. It's all colours and feelings and back-to-front sentences and you often have to ask yourself what on earth they're going on about. But when you've managed to work it all out, it's probably quite clever. I think <u>I'd</u> like to be a poet.

So anyway, I ended up soaking in some gloriously whatsit spring sunshine with Dave. I didn't want to. I wanted to be on my own. Only Dave said, 'Do you want to have lunch with me?' and I couldn't come up with a good excuse not to. I mean, if I'd said, 'No, because I'm Vanishing Man,' he might have thought my brain had been taken over by blobby, alien mind-taker-overers. Which, come to think of it, in my current mood of grimbly grumbliness might not be such a bad thing.

Dave said, 'How's it going?'

I said, 'Fine.'

He said, 'Good.'

I said, 'Yup.'

He said, 'Paul and me are going paintballing with Boys' Brigade this evening. Do you want to come? I'm sure it'd be OK with Greg.'

I said, 'No thanks. Sounds a bit too sporty for me.'

He said, 'Right.'

I said, 'Yeah.'

He asked, 'So, if you're giving up everything even vaguely on the sporty sort of side (which, by the way, I don't think paintballing remotely is), what are you going to do instead? Cross-stitch?'

'I think I'm going to be a poet, if you must know,' I answered.

'A poet,' he nodded crunching into a mouthful of crisps. 'Cool.'

Then he made a face.

'What's wrong with being a poet?' I said.

He shook his head and pointed to his mouth.

'Black pepper crisps. Hot, or what?'

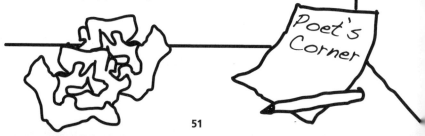

Poet's Corner

I walked into the kitchen and Dad was standing by the sink, staring at his beans. That is to say, he was staring at his yoghurt pots. There's no sign of any beans yet.

'You need to be patient,' said Mum. 'That boy, Jack, may have ended up with a super fast-growing variety, but on the whole I don't think beans tend to shoot up overnight.'

'But that's just it,' said Dad. 'It's been a week.'

'Perhaps you've been overdoing the watering.'

Dad said, 'I just wanted to see something growing.'

'Well, that's easy,' Mum replied. 'Pop round to the allotment and watch the weeds.'

Greg rang.

He said, 'Just been paintballing. You should have come.'

I said, 'No, it's OK. I got to talk about beans with Dad.'

Greg said, 'I didn't know your dad was a gardener.'

I said, 'He's not.'

'Anyway,' Greg went on, 'I just rang to see how you were feeling. Dave says you're still a bit down.'

A bit down? Try wallowing in a pit of grimbly grumbliness. (I knew I could be a poet.)

'No,' I said, 'I'm fine.'

He wants me to mention his polar bear card, I know he does. Well, I'm not going to. Even if <u>he</u> mentions it, I'm not going to say a thing. I didn't ask him to give me a card. I didn't want him to give me a card. He just went out and gave me a card. I'm saying nothing.

'Did you get my card?' Greg asked.

'Yeah, I did, thanks.'

'I meant what I wrote,' he said. 'God loves you so much. Sometimes it's hard to see just how much when things don't go our way, but whatever you think, He'll never leave you.'

Don't. Don't say nice things. Not now. Not on the phone when Mum's in the kitchen probably listening to every sound I make.

'God hasn't gone anywhere,' Greg went on. 'His eternal arms are still in exactly the same place as they were yesterday and as they'll be tomorrow. Right underneath you, supporting you. And He hasn't taken your gifts away. He's got big plans for you, buster, so you'd better get used to it.'

Stop it. Stop talking. My eyes are doing that prickly thing they sometimes do and I can feel a hard sort of lumpiness in my throat. It doesn't mean I'm going to cry or anything. I don't cry. Well, hardly ever. There was that time when I got stung by a wasp when I was about five because it was trying to eat my ice cream and I was trying not to let it, but, I mean, who wouldn't cry if they got stung by a wasp that was trying to eat their ice cream? But nobody cries on the phone. Nobody cries because someone's being nice to them. Especially not when their mum's in the kitchen listening. That would just be, well … cry-babyish.

'I thought God didn't love me any more!' I blurted out.

Just like that. All of a sudden. I couldn't help it. It's the first time I'd said it. I'd been thinking it. Ever since the first-round match. I couldn't <u>stop</u> thinking it. But I'd never said it.

'I thought He was paying me back for being a show-off by making me lose the match. You see, I was going to be a professional footballer, but now it's obvious I'm not good enough, so I'm going to have to be a poet instead and, the worst of it is, I don't know if I'm any good at that either!'

I heard Greg smile. It's weird how you can do that sometimes on the phone. Hear someone smile. I mean normally when you're face to face with someone and they smile, you can see it, but you can't hear it because it's kind of silent. You can hear someone giggle. Or snigger. Or laugh. But not smile. Except sometimes on the phone. You're talking to someone and they smile and somehow you just know.

I knew Greg was smiling when he said, 'Just because you didn't score one goal doesn't mean you're not good at football. Things happen to us. They go wrong. And it can be really tough when they do, especially if something we really want, something we've worked hard for, doesn't work out the way we expected or hoped it would. But it's not God "paying us back" for getting something wrong. It's not God punishing us. Jesus came and got rid of all of that. He took away our punishment for the bad things we do by dying for us. Now we can say sorry to God and know that He forgives us.'

'But I tried so hard,' I burbled, 'and Mr Richardson said I was a natural trolley. I thought being a natural trolley and being God's friend at the same time meant I couldn't lose.'

'Being a Christian doesn't mean always scoring to win the match, Danny. Or being top of the class, or the brainiest brain in Britain. Not everything's going to go fantastically perfectly for us simply because we're Christians. That's not what it's all about. It's about giving ourselves to God. Doing what He asks. Trying to live how He wants us to. And that can be hard. But there's one thing we can be absolutely confident about: God knows what He's doing with our lives. We can trust Him. And, when things don't go according to our plan – because they're not always going to – maybe there's a reason. God could be trying to bring us closer to Him. He could be trying to teach us something. Why not ask Him? You see, when something bad happens, we always have a choice: we can turn away from God and be miserable, or we can <u>choose</u> to see if there's anything good that can come out of it. We can <u>choose</u> to keep talking to God.'

In bed

Mum came in to say good night. At least, that's why she made out she'd come in, but actually I could tell there was more to it.

'You feeling better now?' she began.

'Yeah,' I answered. 'Not that I wasn't feeling all right anyway, of course.'

'Oh, of course,' she nodded.

She was waiting, though. Waiting for me to tell her what happened on the phone. Waiting for me to tell her why I cried (only, of course, I didn't cry because I don't).

'The thing of it is,' I said (well, I had to say something), 'I mean I know you probably won't understand this, but I've been sort of ignoring God since the first-round match, and feeling as if I'm a bit of a useless blob. And it's not nice feeling like that. But Greg says it doesn't have to be that way. It doesn't have to be that way for anybody. He says that whatever happens, we can all choose to keep on talking to God because even when things go badly and, as in my case, the wheels fall off your trolley, He's always there. So that's what I'm going to try and do – keep on talking to Him and eventually I'll probably feel much less … blobby.'

'Mmm,' said Mum. 'Well, I'm glad your church youth leader sorted that out for you.'

'Mmm,' I said.

'Night, night, then,' she added, and I thought she'd gone. But then she put her head back round the door.

'By the way,' she said, 'your dad and me, we really love you, you know. As wombats go, you're pretty special. Blobby or otherwise.'

Lord God, it was me, wasn't it? I was the one who went away, not You. You've been there all the time. You've still been holding out Your arms for me, it's just that I've been ignoring them. I'm sorry I stopped talking to You. I'm sorry I said You've never done anything for me. I didn't mean it, I was just angry. I'm everything I am because of everything You've given to me. Help me to remember that Your way is so much better than my way. Help me to realise that what You want for me is the best – even if it doesn't feel like it. If You've given me stuff to be good at, special talents, I want to try to learn how to use them for You. It's just that … I'm not sure what they are any more. I was going to try and play football for You because I thought that was my gift. But now I don't think it is at all. Now I don't know what I'm good at. And if I do carry on playing football, it might go wrong again. Then people will start staring at me again and wondering how I can possibly be so stupid. So at the moment, I don't really know what I'm going to do for You. Sorry. Amen.

I'll definitely keep on talking to God, but one thing's for sure. There's no point wasting any more time on footie. I'm not going to play again. I'm going to stop doing any sort of sport. If it's not your gift, it's not your gift. And, as far as I'm concerned, I guess it's just not. Besides, maybe giving it all up'll be cool. It's a real slog all that running and star-jumping and press-upping. I'm sure there's loads more exciting stuff I could do than that. Lying in bed, for instance. And poetry-writing, for another instance. I bet there are poets all over the world who started out as sporty people and then turned into poetry-type people. Bound to be.

FRIDAY 24

AM

Dumped my football boots on the breakfast table.

Mum said, 'Do you have to put those there?'

I said, 'Yes. They need to go to a charity shop.'

She said, 'Why? Do they play football in charity shops these days?'

I said, 'No. At least, I don't think so. I'm just not going to be needing them any more.'

'And that would be because ...?'

'Because I'm just not.'

PM

Got home from youth club and Mum was all excited. Dad, on the other hand, wasn't.

'Not a bean shoot in sight,' he grunted. '<u>And</u> I managed to break my new spade.'

'I've met them, Danny,' Mum announced. 'The new people. The ones who moved into the ground floor flat last weekend.'

'What I don't understand is why the ground's so hard,' Dad went on. 'I mean, is it normal to keep breaking spades?'

'I bumped into them in the car park,' Mum said. 'They've got the space opposite us.'

'You see, at this time of year,' Dad explained, 'you'd expect the ground to be quite soft. After all, we're only just out of winter.'

'Well, when I say "them",' Mum added, 'I mean her. Mrs Frobisher. Gilly.'

'And we've had rain,' Dad rambled. 'Lots of rain. The earth should be as soft as … mud.'

'D'you know what,' Mum nattered, 'she is <u>so</u> lovely. Her husband works away quite a bit, so a lot of the time it's just her and the two kids.'

'That's what makes it such a puzzle,' he frowned. 'Unless I'm just buying the wrong sort of spade.'

'There's Josh who's the same age as you,' she smiled, 'and then there's Henry – who's actually a girl (it's short for Henrietta) – and she was six last month.'

'Mind you,' Dad remarked, 'what is the <u>right</u> sort of spade? I mean, spades are all meant for digging, aren't they, otherwise they wouldn't be called spades. A spade is something you dig with.'

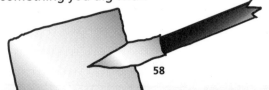

'I could invite them up for tea tomorrow,' Mum suggested, tapping Dad on the head with a teaspoon. 'What do you think?'

'Sorry?' said Dad.

'I said, what do you think?' Mum repeated.

'About what?' asked Dad.

'Inviting them all up for tea tomorrow,' Mum answered.

'Who?' said Dad.

'The Frobishers!'

'Who are the Frobishers?'

'The new people!' Mum snapped. 'Haven't you been listening to a word I've said?'

'Probably,' Dad replied. 'Anyway, why do you want to ask them up for tea? Do they know about spades?'

'What?'

'Spades. For digging.'

'Who in the world said anything about spades?'

I have a feeling this could go on indefinitely. I'm going to go to my room now.

My room

Been thinking about my possible journey into poetryland. (Being a poet, in other words.)

At youth club John said, 'Fancy some table tennis? First to ten wins.'

I said, 'No, thanks. I don't do that any more. But when you look at me, do you ever think, yeah, Danny could be a poet?'

John said, 'To be totally honest ... no.'

'But,' I said, 'is that because you never really think

about poetry or is it because you've never really put me and poetry together?'

John said, 'Is this a trick question?'

'It's just,' I said, 'I think this would be a good time for me to try out some different things. It's not as if I planned to be sporty forever … at all … really.'

'Mmm,' John said.

'So, what do you think?'

'I think you should have some chips.'

'No, I mean about being a poet?'

'Exactly. I think you should have some chips.'

Went into the kitchen to get a drink. Dad was prodding his yoghurt pots.

He asked, 'Do you fancy a trip to the garden centre in the morning? They're doing a special deal on overalls.'

I thought, like what? Buy one pair get a T-shirt with 'Warning – I'm incredibly boring' on it free?

'No, it's all right, thanks,' I said.

'Oh, go on,' he insisted. 'I could get you some as well.'

'Dad,' I said, 'will having overalls make your beans grow?'

'Not necessarily,' he answered, 'but what's wrong with looking the part? Besides, if a thing's worth doing, it's worth doing properly.'

And, apparently, worth wearing overalls.

In bed

I remember Mr Mallory saying once that poets can often be quite complicated people. That's another thing that makes me think perhaps I should try being a poetry-writing person, because I sometimes feel I have quite a complicated life. My parents, for example, make life very complicated.

SATURDAY 25

AM

'They're going to come up,' Mum said.

'Pardon?' I said.

'The Frobishers,' Mum said. 'They're going to come to tea.'

Sometimes Saturday mornings can be wickedly cool. You know, weekend's just beginning. Ages till Monday. Acres of free time, Topz stuff and TV to look forward to. Yup. Saturday mornings are usually ace-in-your-face.

Except <u>this</u> Saturday morning. So far, it's not looking good. Today, my options seem to be:

1. Going with Dad to the garden centre to buy overalls (I'm sorry, but how sad is that?);
OR
2. Helping Mum decide which of her famous cake recipes would produce the most appropriate cake for tea with the Frobishers.

Talk about being spoilt for choice (not).

Mum said, 'I'm in a real quandary. I think I've narrowed it down to chocolate fudge and lemon drizzle, but how I'm supposed to choose between them,

I really haven't a clue. I wish your gran was here. She was a genius at matching a cake to a person.'

***

Sometimes science tests can be a blessing in disguise.

Dad said, 'Danny, are you ready for the garden centre?'

I said, 'Sorry, Dad, but I can't go. I've got a science test to revise for.'

Mum said, 'Danny, you've got to help me decide what cake I'm making otherwise I won't have time to bake it.'

I said, 'Sorry, Mum, but I haven't got time. I've got a science test to revise for.'

Dad said, 'That's the trouble with school these days. It's all tests, tests, tests.'

'Exactly,' said Mum. 'When I was at school, we still had time for a bit of fun at the weekends.'

I thought, fun would be good, but overalls and cake baking? Give me a break.

PM

Been indoors revising for ages – which is a bit of a pig pain because it's sunny.

Paul rang to see if I wanted to go round. He said he'd been cleaning up his bike because it was still plastered in mud from the last Topz cycle ride.

I said, 'That was weeks ago. Didn't you wash it down straight away?'

Paul said excitedly, 'No. I had this incredibly clever idea. I thought that if I left all the mud to dry out really well on the bike, all I'd have to do was tap it a bit and it'd just drop off.'

'Oh,' I said, 'and has it?'

'Well, sort of,' he said. 'A bit. Here and there …
Actually, no, not at all. Do you fancy coming round and
giving me a hand to clean it up?'

I said, 'That sounds really cool, but I've got to revise
for a science test.'

He said, 'Can't you do it later?'

I said, 'No. Believe me, it's got to be now.'

He said, 'Why's that, then?'

I said, 'Please don't make me explain. It'll only remind
me how complicated my life is.'

On the plus side, I now know everything there is to
know in the whole, entire universe (probably) about
food chains and, all I can say is, I'm
really happy not to be an earthworm.

They'll be here soon. The new Frobishers. Well, they're
not new Frobishers, obviously. They've presumably
been Frobishers for as long as they can remember. If
not longer than that. But they're new to us. New to me.
And that's what bothers me.

I'm not good with new people. I don't always know
what to say. Not when it's just me and someone else.
Someone else who doesn't know me. Someone else I've
never met before.

It's different when you're in a group playing football
or something (which obviously I won't be doing any
more). There's a whole group of you to talk about
stuff. A whole group of you to keep all the chat going.
When one person stops, someone else is there to take
over. Sort of like a relay running race (which obviously

I won't be doing any more either). Relay chat is just so not like when it's only one person talking to another person. When the Frobishers come for tea, it'll just be me talking to Josh. I mean, Mum and Dad will be there and Mrs Frobisher will be there. And I suppose what's-her-name, Henry, will be there too. But when it comes to me having to talk, it'll be just me and Josh.

Mum'll say, 'You boys must have so much to talk about.'

And I'll be thinking, no, nothing at all, actually.

Mum'll say, 'It's obvious you two are going to get on like a house on fire.'

And I'll be thinking, obvious to who?

Mum'll say, 'Go on, then, Danny, show Josh your bedroom. I know you're dying to.'

And I'll be thinking, no, I'm not. Why would Josh and me want to be on our own, by ourselves, just him and me, in a completely different room? What on earth are we going to say to each other? WHY DO YOU ALWAYS HAVE TO ASSUME THAT YOU KNOW ME BETTER THAN I KNOW MYSELF??

!!!

I mean, it's not that I'm shy or anything. In fact, I'm not shy at all. Shy people probably feel really awkward around people they don't know, and try anything not to have to be left on their own with them because they never know what to say. Me, I just … feel really awkward around people I don't know and try anything not to have to be left on my own with them because I never know what to say.

> OK, so I'm shy. But, shyness could be a very helpful addition to the whole being complicated thing when I eventually become a poet.

I remember Greg talking about shyness once at Sunday Club. He said that however nervous we may feel about meeting new people, we should always try to remember that they might well be just as worried about meeting us as we are about meeting them. And he said that even <u>not</u> shy people don't always <u>feel</u> like having to chat to people they've never met before. He said that when Jesus was living with us on earth, He was so busy doing all the work He had to do for God that there were probably times when He was very, very tired, and the last thing He would have felt like was being all friendly and chatty. But because Jesus loved everyone so much and wanted them to believe in who He was so that they could be close to God forever, He always took the time to tell them stories, or to help them, or to be welcoming, or to heal sick people who needed healing, or simply to talk. And Greg said that that's what we should try to do whenever we can – be welcoming and friendly.

'After all,' he said, 'for all you know, the person you're nervous about talking to or don't feel like bothering with could be having a really bad day, and God might have sent you to help cheer them up – or even to tell them all about Him.'

In which case:

Thank You, Lord God, for these new people, the Frobishers. Thank You that Mum is being welcoming and friendly, and spent ages this morning baking two different sorts of cake so that they can be lemony or chocolatey when they arrive, depending on how they happen to be feeling. And thank You that Dad is just naturally chatty and will be able to keep them all entertained for hours with his talk of overalls and beans.

But, to be honest, I just really don't want to have to be on my own with any of them in case I don't know what to say. Let's face it, there's nothing welcoming or friendly about sitting in someone's bedroom in total silence. Just the opposite, in fact. Please help me, Lord God. Help me to be like Jesus. Amen.

In bed

Some things are just meant to be, aren't they? That is to say, they couldn't have happened in a more absolutely brain-bogglingly perfect way if you'd sat down and worked them all out beforehand by writing a huge, long list called 'Things that need to happen in order for everything to be absolutely brain-bogglingly perfect, especially when meeting new people'.

Only, of course, I didn't know how to make this afternoon go one way or another. But God did.

It went like this:

3.25pm – Door bell rang.
Mum screamed, 'Aah! They're early! Go and let them in then, Danny.'

I said, 'Why do I have to be the one who lets them in?'

She said, 'Because I haven't quite finished getting the lumps out of my lemon icing and your father's in the bedroom having trouble getting out of his overalls.'

Fantastic, I thought. Not only do I have to be on my own with one new person, I now have to be on my own with three new people. Life doesn't get any easier, does it? (Although, having said that, at least I'm not an earthworm.)

Door bell rang again.

'Danny!' snapped Mum.

'I'm going, I'm going,' I grumbled.

Then I opened the front door.

First I saw Mrs Frobisher.

'Hello,' she smiled. 'You must be Danny.'

Next I spotted Henry. She just looked at me.

Then I noticed Josh.

He grinned, looked me right in the eye and said, 'Hi.'

This is going to be worse than I imagined, I thought. Josh is obviously one of those super-confident people who make shy-with-new-people like me feel like their little toenail.

'Yeah, hi,' I mumbled. 'Come in.'

Mum called from the kitchen, 'I'll be with you in a minute. Go on through.'

Oh no. Mum's 'minutes' can be anything from half an hour to the middle of next week.

I showed the Frobishers into the lounge. That's when I noticed. There was something about the way Josh walked. It looked all awkward. Sort of stiff and jerky, as if having to move was a real effort. I wonder what he's done to his legs, I thought.

'So, Danny,' said Mrs Frobisher, 'I hear you're at Holly Hill Primary School.'

'Yes,' I said.

'I was really hoping there'd be space for Josh and Henry there, but they're all full up for now.'

'Right,' I said.

'Still,' she went on, 'it seems to be all right at Brompton Green, doesn't it?'

'Yeah, it's cool,' Josh said.

Henry still just looked at me. She hadn't stopped just looking at me from the moment I opened the door. Perhaps that's what you do when you're six.

Pause.

'Do you know Brompton Green?' Mrs Frobisher asked.

'Yes,' I answered. (I don't know why. I'd never heard of it.)

Even longer pause.

'Mum'll be in in a minute,' I said. It was all I could think of.

'Is your dad here today?' Mrs Frobisher asked.

'Oh, yes,' I said. 'He should be in in a minute, too. He's just a bit ... caught up in his overalls.' Well, I thought it was best to let them know. There was just the vague possibility that he might be stuck inside them forever, in which case, when he appeared for cake shortly in a complete tangle except for maybe the odd arm or leg flapping free, there'd be no need for any further explanations.

'I expect overalls can be like that,' Mrs Frobisher

nodded understandingly. 'Tricky little things.'

Not half as tricky as this, I thought. Jesus may have been good at talking to complete strangers, but I'm about as much use as a soggy biscuit – rubbish when it comes to the crunch.

Fortunately, this was one of Mum's quick minutes and just then she appeared.

'So sorry to keep you, everybody,' she said. 'You know what it's like when your icing's lumpy. Now, who's for tea and cake?'

4.10pm – All going pretty well, considering. (Considering I have the communication skills of a hard-boiled egg when it comes to meeting new people, that is.) Mind you, pretty much all I had to do at this point was eat cake, hand around the chocolate fingers, and smile in all the right places. Even a hard-boiled egg can do that.

Only, that's when she said it. Mum. Just like I knew she would.

'Go on, then, Danny, show Josh your bedroom. I know you're dying to.'

Sometimes when Mum talks to me, it's a bit like coming face to face with a huge, ugly troll. Not that my mum is huge or ugly, or even troll-like come to think of it, but it's that same feeling of being trapped in a corner by a troll and knowing it's pointless trying to escape because somehow or other, it <u>just won't let you</u>.

I did glance quickly at Dad (who had finally appeared, happily unravelled from his overalls) in case he managed to pick up on my horrified look of 'Oh, no, please don't make me do this'. But, tragically, he was fully occupied in trying to dab chocolate fudge off his shirt without being noticed, so it was a bit of a wasted effort.

However ...

4.15pm – Be prepared to be brain-boggled.

Josh: (IN MY ROOM LOOKING AT MY TROPHY SHELF) Are those all your trophies?

Me: Yeah. (POINTING TO MY FAVOURITE ONE) That's my favourite one. Got it for running.

Josh: I've got a few trophies, too.

Me: Have you? What for?

Josh: Running mostly. I find it quite hard but I really love it.

Me: Is that how you hurt yourself?

Josh: What d'you mean?

Me: Your legs. It looks as if it hurts you to walk.

Josh: Nah, I've got CP.

Me: CP?

Josh: Cerebral Palsy.

Me: What's that?

Josh: Just stuff going on in my brain that affects how I move.

Me: What, all the time?

Josh: Oh, yeah. I have a bit of trouble with my hands, but mostly it's problems with my legs. That's why running's a bit hard.

Me: You still manage to do it, though?

Josh: Of course I still do it. It's my favourite thing.

 I train all year and I run in the Disabled Athletics Championships. Sometimes it doesn't go so well, but that's the same for everybody. It's easier now than it was because I've been to hospital for operations, but you just have to learn to adapt to your own body.

Me: Must be tough, though, when you like doing sport.

Josh: Not really. I mean, it doesn't stop me running. I just get on and do it anyway. Besides, my CP isn't that bad, not compared to some people's. Some people have to be in a wheelchair and they can't even talk. Me, I can talk till the cows go on holiday and, hopefully, I'll always be able to run.

4.30pm – And finally:

Josh was looking across at my bedside table. It's where I keep my Bible.

'Do you read the Bible?' he asked.

I must admit that my stomach did do a bit of a flip at that point. Oh help, I thought. The normal chatty natter's going OK, but I don't know if I'm brave enough to start telling Josh about God yet.

'Yes,' I said quietly.

'What, a lot?'

'Quite a lot. I try to read it nearly … every … well, most … sort of … days.'

'Are you a Christian, then?' he asked.

'Umm … yes.'

'So am I!'

!!!

Sometimes there's so much to get your head around, you feel as though it's going to fall off in the process.

First up, there was me getting in a panic I'd have nothing to talk about with Josh when actually there was loads (I guess because Josh did most of the talking). Second up … there's something niggling at me, right deep inside, and I hate being niggled at. It's as if something's trying to tell me I'm being a real dingbat idiot but I'm not. Josh is Josh and I'm me. And that's all there is to it. So there. Blah de blah.

Lord God, I don't know how You keep doing it. Just when I think I know exactly how something's going to turn out, You go and come up with the mind-bendingly unexpected. Life with You is more full of surprises than a surprise mystery tour – which, being a 'surprise' mystery tour, is guaranteed to be extremely surprising. I mean, I was dreading it this afternoon, having to be all chitty-chatty with complete strangers, but not only does Josh turn out to be mega cool <u>and</u> incredibly easy to talk to <u>and</u> a Christian, he's also the only Christian in his family. That means he's like me. That means he understands how it feels living with parents who don't know You and probably think he's a bit weird because he talks to You and goes to church. (Although how my dad can have the nerve to think anyone's weird when he's the one getting tangled up in his overalls and being excited over planting broccoli, I really haven't a clue.)

Anyway, thank You, Lord God, for Josh. Thank You that now I've got someone to talk to who understands what's it's like to feel a bit on your own sometimes. And thank You that his mum said he could start coming to church with me. Brill baggins, or what? Sunday Club here we come. Amen.

Mum came in to say good night.

She said, 'Are you still scribbling in that thing? You've been writing stuff for hours.'

I said, 'That's because some days there's just hours of stuff to write about.'

I thought for a minute, then, 'Mum,' I said, 'did you know?'

'About what?' Mum asked.

'About Josh having cerebral palsy,' I said.

'His mum mentioned it, yes, but only because she was talking about school.'

'Why didn't you say anything?'

'What's to say?' Mum smiled. 'I didn't bother to tell Josh that you broke your leg a while ago playing football, or that you really hate gooseberries, or that you're a bit of a wombat when it comes to meeting people for the first time. Those things are all a part of who you are, but they're just a small part. And CP is just a small part of Josh. There's so much else to find out. So much else that makes him who he is. Why mention one thing when there are a million others? And probably more than that.'

SUNDAY 26

AM

Going up to Benny's flat in a minute for a lift to church. We're picking Josh up on the way out.

Been thinking about Mum. She's actually pretty cool. She really does accept people simply for who they are, no matter what. Just like God does. And she really seems to love people, too. Just like God does.

Help me to be like that, Lord. Accepting and loving. And help Mum to see how much You accept and love her so that she can begin to accept and love You, and have You as her best friend. Always. Amen.

PM

Walked into church with Josh, and everyone was buzzing around like, 'Who's this?'

I said to Josh, 'Sorry about that. Were the people in your old church this nosey?'

Sarah said, 'It's not nosiness, actually. It's being full of welcomy-ness.'

'Of course it is,' said Josie. 'I mean, you wouldn't want us to ignore Josh, would you? Then you'd be asking, "Were the people in your old church this rude?"'

It was Paul who had to go and say it: 'What's wrong with your legs?'

But Josh was fine about it. He just explained it like he explained it to me.

I said to him later, 'Don't you get fed up with people asking?'

'I suppose I do sometimes,' he shrugged. 'But what's the point? They're still going to ask.'

'So,' said John, 'what do you think of Holly Hill?'

'It's good,' Josh said. 'And you're all Topz, are you?'

'That's us,' grinned Benny. 'You'll get to know who's who really quickly, but just to help you out, Dave's the wise one (well … ish); Sarah's the scatty one.'

'Thanks a lot,' said Sarah.

Very nosey church person

↓

74

'Only trying to be helpful,' said Benny. 'Then there's Paul, the brainy one; John, who's a bit dopey ...'

'What d'you mean, "a bit dopey"?' interrupted John.

'Exactly,' answered Benny. 'You know Danny, obviously. He's the serious one.'

'Serious about sport,' added Josie.

'Serious about lots of things, actually,' I said.

'That's true,' Dave said. 'He's thinking of becoming a poet and it doesn't get much more serious than that.'

'A poet?' said Paul. 'Since when?'

'Since ... I started thinking about becoming one,' I answered.

'That brings us to,' Benny continued, 'Josie, the confident one and, of course, me and I'm the ...'

'Barmy one?' suggested Josh.

'Barmy as a cheese scone!' Benny nodded. 'You're getting the hang of us already.'

After Josh had met Greg and Louise and all the other Sunday Clubbers, Greg asked, 'So, Josh, is there anything we ought to know about you? No secret ambitions to be the next biggest thing in poetry after Danny, for example?'

'No,' smiled Josh. 'Well, not exactly. I do write words for songs sometimes.'

'Really?' said Greg. 'What do you play?'

'Oh, no,' said Josh, 'I don't play an instrument or anything. I just sometimes get tunes in my head so I make up words for them.'

'That is so clever!' gasped Sarah. 'What do you write about?'

'God mostly,' answered Josh. 'When I get a tune going in my head, it's God I start to think about.'

And that's when Josh told us how he became a

Christian. He just sat there in front of all of us – all of us who he hardly knew at all – and explained about it. I mean, how brave is that? Stonkingly brave, that's how. And his story is just, well, gobsmacking.

Josh said that, one time when he was in hospital having another operation on his legs, he was feeling really down and grungy because everything hurt so much, and then he met this girl called Georgie. He wasn't exactly sure what was wrong with her. All she used to say was that she had to go to hospital quite often so that the doctors could change her blood.

Anyway, Georgie was a Christian and she was the one who told him about God – how much He loves us and wants to be our friend and help us get through when things seem really tough. She said she hated having to go into hospital, but she knew that, whatever happened, God would be with her. He'd never leave her, not for one second, because that was what He'd promised. So, when she was feeling scared, she'd tell Him and ask Him to stay especially close. And He always did, she said.

When Josh asked her how she could be so sure, Georgie answered, 'Because of this,' and she showed him a verse in her Bible. It's from the end of Romans chapter 8, and Josh says that now it's his favourite part in the whole book:

'For I am certain that nothing can separate us from his [God's] love: neither death nor life, neither angels nor other heavenly rulers or powers, neither the present nor the future, neither the world above nor the world below – there is nothing in all creation that will ever be able to separate us from the love of God which is ours through Christ Jesus our Lord.'

Georgie told Josh that for her, the 'nothing in all creation' was being ill.

'However bad I feel,' she had said, 'and however many times I have to come into hospital and leave everything at home, like Mallow, my rabbit, and Nibbles (that's my gerbil), none of it can come between me and God. It can all feel horrible but none of it can stop Him loving me. It says so. Right there.'

Josh went on, 'I thought a lot about that, and Georgie lent me her Bible so I could read some more. That's how I found out that all the things we do wrong are called "sins", and our sins make God unhappy, which is why He sent Jesus. God wanted us to be His friends more than anything but, because He is God and God is holy, He had to find a way of getting rid of our sins first. Really, we all should have been punished and never allowed to be anywhere near to Him, but that's not what He wanted. So, instead of us being punished, Jesus died so that He could take our punishment away. Then He came back to life and now He's with God forever. If we believe all that, believe that Jesus is the Son of God, tell God we're sorry for the wrong things we do and give our lives to Him, then when we die, we can be with Him forever too. Only we don't even have to wait till we die. Georgie told me that whenever we give our lives to God, that's the start of our forever with Him.

'So when I realised that, when I really, properly understood it, how could I not give God my life? How could I take no notice after He'd done all that for me?

How could I say no to all that love? I couldn't. So I didn't. And it was amazing! I used to get quite angry and frustrated about having CP. I used to think, why does this have to be me? Why can't I just have legs that work like other people's? Why do I have to be the one everyone stares at and points at because I walk funny? Why can't I just fit in?

'But, after I gave my life to God, all those feelings started to go away because I began to understand that not even something like my CP can stop Him loving me. And if it doesn't bother Him, how can I let it bother me? So now if I see people looking at me, or hear them say something mean, I just think <u>they're</u> the ones with the problem and I don't get angry any more. It can still hurt me but I know now that it's how God feels about me that matters.'

Everyone was quiet when Josh had finished. It was so incredible what he'd said. I mean, we all know what God's done for us, but there was just something about the way Josh explained it. It was all so real to him. So exciting. Maybe sometimes when you've been a Christian for a while, you and God, it's just the way it is. Just everyday sort of stuff. Maybe you even start to take it for granted. But the way Josh talked to us about it, the way you could see that God really was his very best friend and had made all the difference in the whole, enormous, wide world to him, it kind of made your brain want to explode. God's love for us is just so mega. So <u>MASSIVE.</u> And so real.

Looking at Josh in Sunday Club, seeing how much God means to him and how much knowing Him has changed his life, made me never want to take God for granted ever again.

Josh gave me the words to one of his songs. He'd typed it out on his laptop.

'I have to type,' he grinned. 'My handwriting looks as if an earwig wrote it.'

'You should see mine,' I said. 'I mean, I can read it but Mr Mallory, my teacher, says that to anyone else it's an uncrackable code.'

'Oh,' said Josh. 'Cool.'

Josh's Song

You are God, You are holy,
But You called to me.
I was sad, I was angry,
Then You set me free.

Now I want to SHOUT about You,
Let the wide world see
How You changed my life
And with Your love You set me free.

Thank You for my legs to run with,
For my whole body.
Thank You that Your love's forever.
Reaching even me.

Come on, everybody, listen!
Take a look at me.
Now I'm like a brand-new person.
God has set me free.

What can I say? Brilliant. Just brilliant.

That niggle's still there. It's getting worse. Josh is so great but being around him is making me feel niggled. What's that all about? If I want to give up football, I'll give up football. It's <u>my</u> choice. (The really weird thing is Josh hasn't even mentioned football.)

MONDAY 27

AM

Door bell rang before breakfast.
It was Benny. He doesn't often come round before breakfast. Especially not on Mondays. He seemed very excited, though, which I realised when he started flapping his arms around and almost poked my eye out.

'Whoops!' he said. 'Anyway, you know what Josh said about nothing coming between him and God? Well, have you been thinking what I've been thinking?'

'I don't know,' I said. 'What have you been thinking?'

'About football,' he said.

Sometimes Benny's outburstings can be a bit random, I've noticed.

'No,' I said. 'Why would I be thinking about football?'

(OK, OK, so I <u>have</u> been thinking about football a bit, but that's beside the point.)

'Because,' Benny explained, 'there's no reason why you should give it up. Even when you were getting a bit … well, sorry, but full of yourself over being a natural and everything, God was still loving you. He was just waiting for you to realise that He's the One who's made you the way you are so it's important to thank Him for the things you're good at and not get bigheaded about them. Just like Greg said. And that goes for me, too.

What I'm trying to say is that God is <u>so</u> much bigger than we think He is. There's nothing on the planet or anywhere in all the entire, whole universe, not even football, that can get in the way of His love for us if we've given our lives to Him. It's like this huge, fiery, burning, zappy beam that just powers right through anything in its path to make sure it reaches us. I mean, if that's not stonkingly megatastic, then I'm a potato. Which I'm not, obviously. At least I hope it's obvious.'

Got to go. Mum says the bus'll be here in a minute. Benny may be a bit of a mad arm-flapper sometimes, but he's right, isn't he, Lord God? He's right about the way You love us. So thank You for Your huge, fiery, burning, zappy beam of love. It <u>is</u> powerful enough to reach us no matter what. And thank You for Josh, too. I don't know if I can ever be brave the way he is – brave enough to be as honest as he was about himself yesterday at Sunday Club, and about what You've done for him – but I'm going to try never to forget how amazing You are. That's what Josh has – amazement. At You and at how much You love him. It's just there in his face and how he talks. Thank You that he's come to live here. I don't think I'll ever forget yesterday. Sunday 26 April. I'm going to call it Amazing Sunday from now on, because that's what You turned it into. Amen.

There's one thing Benny's not right about, though: why I've given up football and all things sporty. It's got nothing to do with God. It's got nothing to do with anything. I've just given them up, that's all.

PM
Sat next to Benny on the bus.

He said, 'I'm not being funny but you don't think I look like a potato, do you?'

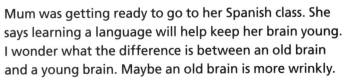

Mum was getting ready to go to her Spanish class. She says learning a language will help keep her brain young. I wonder what the difference is between an old brain and a young brain. Maybe an old brain is more wrinkly.

Before she went out Mum said, 'I'm so glad you and Josh are hitting it off. I knew you would. You're like two peas in a pod, I reckon.'

Dad said, 'Did someone mention peas? Now there's a thought. They could be my next challenge.'

***

I wonder if there's a cure for vegetable mania.

!!!

Josh rang.

Apart from the fact that Josh ringing me was ultra cool, it was also mega relief-making. It meant I could escape from Dad and his fiendish plot to build a shed on his allotment.

I said, 'Paul's dad's got a shed.'

Dad said, 'I know. I've been to see it. He showed me round.'

'He showed you round?' I repeated. 'Paul's dad showed you round his garden shed?' (I thought it might make more sense if I said it. It didn't.)

'It was very nice, actually,' Dad said. 'Good size. With windows.'

'Funky,' I said.

'And shelves.'

'Triffic.'

'Paul's dad says to let him know when I'm going shed shopping and he'll come with me. Help me pick the right one.'

That was when Josh rang.

'I'd better get the phone,' I said.

'Not only that but he's going to come over and put some shelves in it for me,' Dad went on.

'I'm just going to get the phone now.'

'He's a bit of a DIY nut apparently,' Dad rambled.

'I've gone.'

Josh had two things to say on the phone:

Number 1: 'You know there's a prayer team at your church? That group of people who stay behind after the service to pray with anyone who feels they need someone to pray with? Well, I was wondering, has there ever been anything like that for Sunday Club? Only, when you're a kid, it's always great when an adult prays with you about stuff, but sometimes it's good if you can pray with someone your own age. Someone who might even have exactly the same stuff going on as you. If you think it's a good idea, we could maybe mention it to Greg. And then, you and me, perhaps we could start up a Sunday Club prayer team.'

Number 2: 'I won't be here next weekend. I'm going up to see the motor racing with Dad. We go on Saturday, camp overnight at the circuit and come back on Sunday. And I was just wondering (because Dad's fine with it and everything) if maybe you'd like to come too. There's plenty of room in the tent. The racing'll be terrific and we'll be able to go and meet some of the drivers and get their autographs before it starts. I'm sure you'll like it. There are lots of burger stands and they all do wicked chips.'

I had two things to say to Josh:

Number 1: 'Totally, stonkingly, fantastically brilliant! I don't know why we haven't thought of it before. A Sunday Club prayer team would be just ace-in-your-face! Greg's going to love it, I know he is. I'll talk to the Gang, see what they think, and then ring him up.'

Number 2: 'Totally, stonkingly, fantastically brilliant! I mean, I love car racing. I watch it on TV sometimes with Dad (although, oddly, he's a bit more into gardening at the moment) but we've never been to a real life event. How crazy would that be! So you bet your ear lobes I'd like to come with you. Thanks, Josh. I'll start packing my stuff.'

!!!

I said to Mum, 'You're sure it's OK if I go with Josh next weekend?'

Mum said, 'It's fine. I might even give myself a treat and check how clean you've been keeping your room.'

I said to Dad, 'You're sure it's OK if I go with Josh next weekend?'

Dad said, 'Of course it's OK. It's just ...'

'What?'

'You won't be here when I get my new shed.'

I sighed. 'Sadly, no.'

TUESDAY 28

PM

Dave and Benny wanted to play Topz Rules footie at lunchtime but I said we couldn't because I was calling an emergency Topz meeting behind the changing rooms to talk about Josh's idea for a Sunday Club prayer team. Everyone was there except John. He's off school with an ear infection. Sarah says she got woken up by the sound of him moaning in the next room and she thought there was a wild cow in the house – which, considering there are no cows, wild or otherwise, living anywhere near here, she found rather surprising.

'They do hurt, though, ear infections,' said Josie. 'I had one once.'

Sarah said, 'Well, I've had one twice but I didn't lie in bed making wild cow noises.'

Dave said, 'I've had ear infections. Quite a few actually. Apparently I've got narrow channels or something.'

MOO!

Benny asked, 'Do they make you moo?'

'Not moo exactly,' Dave answered, 'but, according to Mum, I have been known to thrash about like a crocodile.'

'I like crocodiles,' said Paul. 'There's a huge one at the zoo. They called it something posh beginning with Z but I think it looks more like a Boris.'

'Er, do you think we could get on with the meeting now?' I said.

Paul said, 'What meeting?'

Ugh.

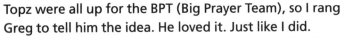

Topz were all up for the BPT (Big Prayer Team), so I rang Greg to tell him the idea. He loved it. Just like I did.

He said, 'I don't know why we haven't thought of it before.' Just like I did.

I said, 'So, shall we do it then?'

Greg said, 'I think first of all we should tell everyone at Sunday Club what Josh would like to do and then pray about it altogether.'

'But why?' I said. 'It's a brilliant idea. Why can't we just do it?'

Greg said, 'If we're going to start up something like this, we have to make sure God's right at the centre. That means we have to be absolutely certain He wants it to happen and we have to be absolutely certain that we end up with the right team members.'

'How long's that going to take?' I said. 'I thought we could just get on with it. I've got this dead cool idea for a poster to let everyone know it's going on. Shall

I tell you about it? It's going to have a photo of each team member on it with their name and age written underneath, and I thought it could have a whopping great title across the top all in different colours:

SUNDAY CLUB'S
BIG PRAYER TEAM

What d'you think?'

'Sensational,' said Greg.

'So, when can we do it?'

'Just as soon as we've told everybody and given it properly to God, which we can start to do altogether when we meet up on Sunday.'

'But Josh and me, we're away this weekend to see the motor racing,' I moaned. 'That means not being able to give it to God until the Sunday after, which is ages away.'

'It really isn't,' smiled Greg. 'In any case, there's nothing to stop you and Josh starting to pray about it right now.'

'So you're saying we could actually have the Big Prayer Team up and running really soon,' I suggested hopefully.

'I'm saying,' said Greg, 'that we need to spend a bit of time giving it to God before we do any more. There's no need to rush into it. Just be patient. Believe me, God's always worth waiting for.'

I hate waiting. It's so pointless and … waiting-aroundy. I'm just not a waiting-aroundy type of person. I'm much more the 'let's get going and do it now' sort. Like Dad, I suppose. Mum reckons he's got ants in his pants. Well, all I can say is, some of them must have escaped into mine. Dad's always leaping around and saying things like, 'Come on then, let's get cracking! No point letting the grass grow under your feet.'

Mind you, he'll be lucky to see the grass grow under anyone's feet in his weedy old allotment.

***

I am SO busy. I've got all my packing to do for the motor racing this weekend, which is bound to take ages because you have to think really carefully about packing and stuff. Supposing you rush it, for instance, and then find you've forgotten something incredibly important like your pyjamas, or you've only put one spare sock in your bag. How much of a disaster would that be!

Then, of course, there's all the praying that needs to be done for the BPT, not to mention organising who's going to do it with who – and when. (Admittedly that side of it will be easier to sort out when I know who's actually going to be on the team, but, hey, you can never start too early with these things.)

On top of all that, Mr Mallory says we're going to be doing a creepy-crawly project (including making a huge, great, long caterpillar to go round the walls of the whole classroom) and we've each got to choose one particular creepy-crawly to find out about. I mean, how much time is that going to take? Loads, that's how much. There are so many creepy-crawlies to choose from. Obviously I'm going to want to pick exactly the right one that combines incredibly interesting living habits with being incredibly interesting-looking, and that could take totally ages. I might even have to start hanging around Dad's allotment and see what I can find scuttling about in the weeds.

And then, of course, there's my poetry writing. I really must do some.

So, all I can say is, it's a good job I've given up football, otherwise I'd never have time to fit everything in.

Went round to Josh's to update him on the BPT. He said we could pray about it now if I wanted to, so we did.

I said, 'Since we're praying together at the moment anyway, maybe we could pray for our parents, too. In fact every time we get together to do BPT praying, we could pray for our parents. That way God will see how much we want them to get to know Him. Greg says people should be really serious about what they're praying for, so let's get serious!'

Josh said, 'Speaking of being serious, and knowing how seriously you're into sport, I was wondering if you'd like to be my running partner? I haven't done that much running since we moved here, but I thought I could start doing laps round the park every day before school. What d'you think?'

'I think it's a great idea,' I said, 'only ... I sort of don't do sport any more.'

'But all your trophies,' Josh said. 'I thought you did loads.'

'I did do loads,' I said. 'I just don't now.'

'Right,' said Josh. 'Why's that then?'

'Because … I'm so busy. And that's just the way it is.'

!!!

Well, it is just the way it is.

And that's that.

WEDNESDAY 29

AM

I expect Josh is out running now. Round the park. Like I used to. It was cool that he asked me to be his running partner. I'd have really liked to do that if it hadn't been now. Because now, obviously, I've given up running and football and all that sort of stuff. Which is fine because, as it turns out, I'm going to be far too busy for it anyway.

PM

On the bus Benny said, 'What's going on?'

I said, 'What's going on with what?'

Benny said, 'You and football. We've been on the field all lunchtime. You're still not playing.'

I said, 'So? It's up to me if I play or not.'

He said, 'But I thought that was all sorted. I thought you knew football wasn't going to get in the way of you and God.'

'It's got nothing to do with me and God,' I said. 'I've just got other things.'

'What other <u>things</u>?' Benny said. 'Sport was your <u>thing</u> and now you're not doing any of it. Why?'

'Because …' I said (realising that it's actually very hard to finish a sentence beginning with 'because' when you've got nothing to finish it with), 'because, Benny … Oh, just <u>because</u>, all right?'

Niggle, niggle, niggle. Everyone's out to get me.

***

Had supper then Dad said, 'Right, Danny. You're coming with me to measure up the allotment for my shed.'

Like I say, everyone's out to get me.

THURSDAY 30

PM

Mum took me out to get some new trainers for the motor-racing weekend and we bumped into Josh in the car park.

I said, 'Hi, Josh, how was the running this morning?'

'OK,' he said. 'A few starers, but OK.'

'Starers?' I said. 'What d'you mean "starers"?'

'People who stare,' said Josh. 'Because of the way I run. It's fine, though. I still did six laps which wasn't bad considering I haven't been out much for a while.'

Why do we do that? Stare at people who are different? It's potty really. I mean, there are so many different sorts of people everywhere, you'd think different would be normal. It's not like that, though. Instead, we stare when we shouldn't, and we poke fun, and it's all wrong. Like Josh says, if it doesn't bother God then why should it bother us?

I felt as if the whole world was staring at me when I missed that goal in the Squad match – and it was just a stupid little goal. It hurt me, though. It really hurt me. It made me feel I wasn't good enough. It made me feel I stuck out like a gooseberry on an apple tree.

It's made me stop playing football.

!!!

Rang Josh.

I said, 'I'm sorry not to be your running partner. If I'd been with you, maybe people wouldn't have stared.'

'Nah,' said Josh. 'They'd have stared anyway. It's what people do.'

'How come you still go out running, then?' I asked. 'How come it doesn't bother you?'

'It <u>does</u> bother me,' said Josh, 'but I can't let it get to me, can I? Otherwise I'd never go anywhere or do anything. Besides, these days I can talk to God. Every time I set foot outside my front door I ask Him to walk with me, and every time I set foot outside my front door, He does. So whenever I'm out I'm not on my own.'

We sing this song at Sunday Club. It's about having faith in God, trusting Him in everything we do. It goes, 'Faith as small as a mustard seed can move mountains.'

Josh has got real, big, serious stuff going on with his CP, but he doesn't let it get in the way of him living his life or doing what he wants to do.

Josh's faith moves mountains every day.

MAY
FRIDAY 1

PM

Mr Richardson came to assembly this morning. He stood up the front going on about some after-school football training club he's starting. It was the first time I'd seen him since the Squad mess-up and I had to make sure he didn't spot me, which would have been hideously hideous. Fortunately I was sitting behind Dave who's quite tall so, by sort of slouching forward and sucking my head down between my shoulders, I managed to hide quite brilliantly I thought.

However, no amount of head-sucking-down could help when I was talking to Paul later outside the cloakroom and Mr Richardson walked by. It's hard to disappear behind someone who's shorter than you are.

'Danny,' Mr Richardson said, 'how's it going?'

'Good,' I spluttered.

'Hope you'll be signing up for the after-school club,' he went on.

'Um … '

'I need dedicated players like you to spur the younger ones on.'

'Er … '

'A few more well-oiled trolleys and we'll have a squad to end all squads next year.'

'The thing is …' I began, but then Benny popped up.

'The thing is,' Benny said, 'haven't you heard? Danny's given up football. For good.'

No time for youth club tonight. Too busy getting ready for the trip tomorrow. It's like I said to Benny, 'If you had as much important stuff going on in your life as I have, playing football wouldn't even come into it.' (I also said, 'Anyway, what I do or don't do is none of your business, so why don't you just GET OFF MY BACK?', which I wish I hadn't now, but there are times when you just can't help yourself.)

After Benny had finished storming off, Paul said, 'Wow! You should so not be giving up footie. Even Mr Richardson still thinks you're the bee's fleas.'

I said, 'It's knees not fleas.'

Paul said, 'It could be fleas, though.'

I said, 'No, it couldn't. Bees don't have fleas.'

Paul said, 'How do you know? I've seen one scratching before.'

***

Mum said, 'You all packed up, then?'

'Yup,' I said.

'I don't know what you were worrying about,' she went on. 'You've still got plenty of time to get to youth club.'

'No, I haven't,' I said. 'There's more to going camping for the weekend than just packing up, you know.'

'Like?'

'Like … a lot of things actually. You just don't realise because you never go camping.'

Josh came round with his dad to make sure I was all set for an early getaway in the morning. I said, yes, I was.

Then Josh said, 'If you're going to that youth club later, Dad says he can give us a lift.'

I said, 'No, I'm not.'

Josh said, 'Why's that?'

I said, 'Because I've got to get all set for tomorrow.'

Josh said, 'I thought you just said you <u>were</u> all set for tomorrow.'

'Yes, I am,' I said. 'But sometimes you need to be more than all set, don't you think?'

!!!

Why do things have to get so complicated? If I'd never been good at football, none of this would be a problem. I could have given it up and no one would have cared. As it is, I've got niggling going on in my head, Mr Richardson breathing down my neck, Mum wondering what she's been missing all these years by not getting out camping, and I'm not going to youth club so that I don't have the whole of Topz ganging up on me about sport. Is life fair? I THINK NOT.

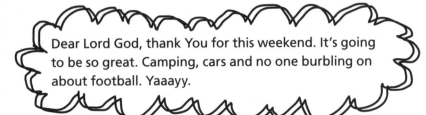

Dear Lord God, thank You for this weekend. It's going to be so great. Camping, cars and no one burbling on about football. Yaaayy.

SATURDAY 2

AM

6.00 – Just off.

Dad said, 'All ready to go?'

I said, 'You bet.'

Mum said, 'Hope it's a comfortable tent.'

I said, 'Mum, comfort and camping don't really go together.'

Dad said, 'Shed'll be here when you get back.'

I said, 'Groovy.'

SUNDAY 3

PM

9.00 – Back home.

Dad said, 'How was the racing?'

I said, 'Totally, trifficly stonking!'

Mum said, 'How was the tent?'

I said, 'Totally, trifficly cool!'

Dad said, 'Bet you can't wait to see the shed.'

I said, 'Bet I can.'

Trifficly stonking!

Trifficly cool!

TUESDAY 5

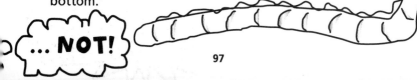

Seriously interesting caterpillar ...

AM

The thing about having faith in God is, I guess you never really know how strong it is until something comes along to test it.

PM

Some days are just made for Topz tattle (ie Topz tattling to each other about stuff they've done, stuff they want to do and stuff they're going to do). Today is definitely a Topz tattle day. It's just unfortunate it also happens to be a Tuesday and therefore a school day, which means we had to save most of our tattling for lunch time, and waiting around for tattle time all morning was actually really hard – especially as it was Bank Holiday yesterday and I was out with Mum and Dad so I still hadn't been able to tell any Topzies about the racing. I was bursting with news of whizzing cars and super-cool racing drivers, and how not to let your tent being flooded in the middle of the night (because the heaviest rainstorm you ever camped in in all your life fell out of the sky) spoil ANY of it. And instead of being able to talk about it all morning, I had to try to be deeply and seriously interested in Mr Mallory's wall caterpillar idea. How tragic is that?

When we finally got let out for lunch, John (who no longer sounds like a wild cow because his ear infection is better) said, 'Come on then, Danny. We want to hear everything. From beginning to end, start to finish and top to bottom.'

Sarah said, 'You can't hear something from top to bottom.'

... NOT!

97

John said, 'Well, I can. You're obviously not listening properly.'

Josie said, 'Exactly how do you listen to something from top to bottom?'

John said, 'Don't you know anything?'

Sarah said, 'Obviously not.'

Dave said, 'When I'm listening, I always find it helps to stop talking first.'

Silence.

'So, Danny,' said Dave, 'how was the racing?'

'Unbelievable!' I exploded. 'To start with, we put the tent up in this huge field right close to the circuit.'

'Really?' said Josie. 'Does that mean you could watch the racing from your tent?'

'No,' I said, 'it wasn't that close.'

'That's a shame,' said Sarah. 'I think that would have been really nice – you know, watching the cars whizzing by while sitting round your little campfire.'

'Cool,' I said. 'Anyway, then we had a walk around and it made you really hungry because everywhere you went you could smell burgers cooking on all the burger stands.'

'Sounds like my kind of place,' said Benny.

'My kind of place would have more doughnut stands than burger stands,' said Sarah.

'Then,' I went on, 'we went to this big open-air bit called the paddock where you could look at all the cars before the racing started, and go and meet the drivers and get their autographs.'

'Wow!' said Paul, and his eyes looked really massive behind his glasses. 'You actually got to meet the drivers and get their autographs?'

'Do they have doughnut stands there, though?' Sarah asked. 'Because if they don't, I think they really should have. There must be lots of people like me who like doughnuts more than burgers and it could put them off going.'

'The cars just boggle your mind,' I said. 'Josh's dad took loads of photos of us standing next to them with the bonnets up so you could see the engines and everything.'

'And what if the drivers want doughnuts?' Sarah continued. 'Imagine being a driver about to drive in a really fast race and what you fancy more than anything else in the world is a doughnut. How would you feel if you got told, "Sorry, we only do burgers."?'

'Sarah,' I said, 'what on earth are you babbling on about?'

'Doughnuts,' she said. 'Isn't it obvious?'

Got in from school and Mum said, 'I've washed your sleeping bag.'

'Thanks,' I said.

Mum said, 'It seemed to be full of mud.'

'I know,' I said. 'That was because of the flood.'

Mum said, 'And you're trying to tell me that camping is fun?'

'Just because something's muddy doesn't mean it's not fun,' I said.

Although I'm not so sure when it comes to Dad's allotment.

***

It was weird today. No one mentioned football. Not even Benny, which is odd because Benny's always mentioning football.

Rang Greg about the BPT. He said they'd all talked about it at Sunday Club and everyone agreed it was a sensational idea. The next thing to do was work out some rules.

'Rules?' I said. 'Since when did praying for people need rules?'

'The thing is,' said Greg, 'if someone's coming to us to ask for prayer, they need to know that what they tell us will stay between us and God, and that we're not going to go off and talk about it to anybody else. So we have to have a rule that we keep what other children tell us private and promise not to gossip about it.'

'Sounds fair,' I said.

'The other thing is,' said Greg, 'that sometimes children can have problems that are really too big for other children to know how to deal with, and an adult needs to be involved. So, Louise and I are going to be part of the team. When someone comes up and asks for prayer, we'll be there too. Louise is a great Sunday Club leader, and she can be with the girls while I'm helping out with the boys. We'll leave the praying to you, but we'll be there to listen and support you.'

That's not quite how I imagined it would be, but if anyone knows how to do things right, it's Greg. Greg seems to know pretty much most things.

'OK,' I said. 'I'll tell Josh.'

I thought for a minute, then, 'Greg,' I said.

'Yes?' he said.

'Nothing.'

Something weird happened.

I was watching TV when Mum came in and sat next to me. I mean, she often comes and sits next to me when I'm watching TV, that's not the weird part. But, after a moment, she fished around in her pocket and pulled out a piece of folded paper which turned out to be the words to Josh's song.

'Mum,' I said, 'that's mine. What are you doing with it?' I was a bit embarrassed, to be honest.

'I found it under your bed,' she told me, 'when I was hoovering. Did you write it?'

'No,' I laughed. 'I can't write stuff like that. Although I might be able to one day when I'm a poet. It's Josh's.'

'Josh's?' Mum said. 'You mean Josh wrote this about God?'

'Yeah,' I said. 'It's good, isn't it?'

And this is the weird part. Mum just carried on sitting

next to me staring at the words on the paper. She didn't say they were silly, or call me a wombat, or come out with anything like I thought she might say.

Instead she just nodded and said, 'I think it's absolutely beautiful.'

My room

Lord God, most of the time chatting away to You is really simple. We can do it any time, anywhere, about anything. The hard part can be hearing You talk back to us. Greg says we have to take the time to listen to You really carefully so that we can get close to You and find out what You're saying to us, like with the BPT. But maybe, just maybe, there are other times when Your voice is so clear that we'd have to be sitting with our heads stuck inside a giant marshmallow, or something, not to be able to hear it. Happily, today my ears are completely free of marshmallow because I heard Your voice just now, I'm sure I did, and You weren't even talking to me. I think You just spoke to my mum.

WEDNESDAY 6

AM

Dad was having breakfast.

I said, 'Dad, I need to go down and see Josh.'

Dad said, 'At this time in the morning? It's a bit early.'

I said, 'No, it's not. All the Frobishers get up early. Josh says so.'

Dad said, 'You could go round after school. Can't it wait till then?'

'No!' I said. 'It's got to be now.'

!!!

Rang Josh's door bell. His mum answered. Henry was hanging onto the sleeve of her jumper and just stood there looking at me. Again.

'Sorry, Danny,' said Josh's mum, 'you just missed him. He's gone to do his laps round the park, but if you run you should catch him.'

Bother, I thought. I'd forgotten about Josh's running. OK, so if I run I'll catch him. But then he'll be wanting to carry on running his laps. Which means I'll have to carry on running to keep up with him so that I can tell him what I need to tell him. Which all seems incredibly complicated, especially as I've given up doing any sort of sporty stuff like running and I haven't even got the right trainers on.

In the end, it has to be said that some things are more important than the right trainers. I shot down the park and caught up with Josh on his third lap.

'Hey, Danny!' grinned Josh. 'I thought you'd given up all this sport malarkey.'

'I have,' I said. 'This doesn't mean a thing. I'm not even wearing the right trainers. What it is, though, is Mum.'

Josh said, 'Don't tell me she wants to come running with me.'

'Don't be daft,' I said. 'The only running Mum ever does is up and down the stairs when the lift's not working. No, it's your song.'

'What song?'

'The one you gave me at Sunday Club.'

'Oh, that song. What about it?'

We ran past two ladies walking a dog. They were both looking at Josh. Even the dog seemed to be looking at Josh. I glanced at him.

'Starers,' he shrugged. 'What about my song?'

'Mum found it in my room,' I said. 'I didn't mean her to or anything, she just found it. And the thing is, she really loved it.'

'Yeah?' smiled Josh.

'Yeah,' I said. 'So the other thing is, I think God might have spoken to her. In fact I'm sure God spoke to her. So the <u>other</u> other thing is, we have to pray for her. Today. Really a lot. Because if He spoke to her last night, she might still be thinking about Him today. Which means that when He speaks to her again she might be more ready to listen to Him.'

'Cool,' said Josh. 'Love your faith, Danny.'

<u>What</u>?

I stopped running.

'What did you say?' I said.

'I love your faith,' he repeated. 'You pray and you believe. Haven't you heard? Faith like that moves mountains! Come on, race you home.'

PM

I said to John, 'Have you chosen a creepy-crawly for Mr Mallory's project yet?'

'No,' he said. 'I wish we were doing lizards. I like lizards.'

'I think lizards ought to be included in any project about creepy-crawlies,' I said. 'After all, there must be lots of people who think lizards are extremely creepy-crawly.'

'That's exactly what I said to Mr Mallory,' John said, 'but he told me it wouldn't fit in with the "overall execution of his master plan and on this occasion he'd have to remain stringently inflexible".'

'Pardon?' I said.

'That's exactly what I said to Mr Mallory,' John said.

Benny asked, 'Have you chosen a creepy-crawly for Mr Mallory's project yet?'

I said, 'No, have you?'

He said, 'Yeah. D'you want to know what it is?'

I said, 'Yeah.'

He said, 'A stick insect. D'you want to know why?'

I said, 'Yeah.'

He said, 'Because it's just like me – thin, stick-like, easy to look after and would make a very good pet.'

***

At home time, Josie said, 'By the way, Mr Richardson was in earlier. He was looking for you.'

'Why?' I said.

'To see if he could put your name down for the after-school football tomorrow.'

'But I'm not doing the after-school football tomorrow. He knows I'm not doing the after-school football tomorrow.'

'That's what I told him,' Josie said. 'But I did say that having it after school on a Wednesday was brilliant because band practice is on a Thursday, so if you changed your mind and decided you <u>were</u> going to do it, it wouldn't get in the way of band practice. On the other hand, if you didn't change your mind and carried on deciding you <u>weren't</u> going to do it, band practice wouldn't stop you doing that either.'

Huh???

Sometimes the things Josie says make about as much sense as hanging upside down from a tree with a banner saying 'I'm confused' wrapped around your ankles.

I'm confused

In fact, I may as well be hanging upside down from a tree. There's so much going on inside my head at the moment it's difficult to know which way round my brain is.

And I'm beginning to feel extremely sick.

Sometimes there's nothing for it but to do some trumpet practice.

***

They're all going to pray. All of Topz. For Mum. It's one of those 'get cracking and don't let the grass grow under your feet' times. If God did speak to Mum through Josh's song yesterday, He needs to know that we want Him to keep on speaking to her. So we've got to keep on speaking to Him. And it should all be so

stonking and triffic.

So why do I feel as if I'm hanging upside down from a tree?

My room ~~~~~~~~~~~~

I said to Dad, 'When you go over to the allotment, please could you drop me round at Greg's?'

Dad said, 'Yes, super. I'll give you a tour of my new shed on the way.'

I sat on the sofa in Greg's kitchen. I like Greg's sofa. It's all soft and snugly, and just worn-looking enough to make you feel it wouldn't matter if you forgot you weren't at home and accidentally slid your feet up onto the cushions.

'So,' said Greg, 'what's all this about hanging upside down from a tree?'

'I don't know,' I said. 'It's just how I feel. I've got this niggle going on inside me all of the time and it won't go away.'

'A niggle, eh?' he said. 'Don't you just hate those? When did it start?'

'When I met Josh,' I told him. At least, that's when I first really noticed it. But actually it was there before I met Josh. It's been there ever since I decided to give up football. And I had to give up football because it's something I've always made out I'm really good at, and you can't have people thinking you're really good at something and then go and let them down like I did in the first-round Squad match, can you? Not only that, but messing up makes you feel like a total dork, with people pointing at you and sniggering behind your back, and who wants to feel like a total dork for the rest of their life? I'd rather never do anything remotely sporty ever again than risk that. So that's what I decided – never to do anything remotely sporty <u>ever</u> again. (Except for PE at school, obviously. Everyone has to do PE.)

Only then I met Josh. And that's when the niggle really got going. Josh has real big stuff to deal with. He's had to go to hospital a lot. He's always going to find it hard work walking. He's probably always going to be stared at. But he's found a way not to let it get him down. He's made friends with God. He asks God to be close to Him and he's absolutely sure that God will always be there, and that's what helps him to go out running. It doesn't matter how much he has to push himself, or how much it hurts, or who's standing staring, he still goes and runs. And he loves it. But me? I've given up what I love because I'm ... scared. Scared of getting it wrong again. Scared of failing. Josh's faith has made him brave. Mine hasn't.

'So what I've been thinking is,' I said, 'maybe I don't have proper faith at all.'

'Do you talk to God?' Greg asked.

'Yes, of course I do,' I said. 'I talk to Him all the time.'

'What do you talk to Him about?'

'Everything. Stuff going on at school. Stuff going on at home. I've been praying specially for Mum. God spoke to her, I know He did, so I've been asking Him to keep on speaking to her and for her to keep on hearing Him.'

'When you talk to God,' Greg said, 'do you think He's listening?'

'I <u>know</u> he's listening,' I frowned, 'otherwise why would I bother talking to Him?' Duh.

'And do you believe He'll answer your prayers one way or another, even if the answer turns out to be no?' Greg asked.

'What do you think?' I answered. 'Yes.' And what's with all the questions?

That's when I noticed Greg was smiling.

'What?' I demanded.

'Sounds an awful lot like proper faith to me,' he said.

Apparently, I'm like a house. Greg says that when someone decides to build a house for themselves, it doesn't happen, just like that. There's lots of work to do. The ground has to be got ready, and big trenches dug out for the foundations, which is what the walls are built on. Then the bricks have to be laid just right to make the walls straight and strong, and there have to be windows in all the best places so that the light can get in and people can see out. And finally, all over the top, there has to be a roof to keep out the wind and the rain, as well as the snow in winter (because playing outside in the snow is wicked, but having it in your house would be nippy to say the least, and not very nice at all).

Greg says that when we ask God to come into our lives, we're like a house being built. We don't turn instantly into the most fantastic Christians on the planet, because there's so much we need to learn and, even then, we'll never be perfect, because only Jesus was perfect. But, if we ask Him to, just like a house God will build us up a little bit more every day, step by step, brick by brick.

Greg says that even if our faith only feels like a tiny speck, it's still faith, and the more we learn to trust in

God, the more that tiny speck of faith will grow, straight and strong, like the walls of a house. But it won't happen unless we give ourselves a push. Unless we put our trust in God and then go for it. Which is what Josh has done. Josh hasn't said to himself, 'Yes, I believe God listens to me when I talk to Him and, yes, I believe He'll be with me when I go out running,' and then just sat around indoors. He's been brave enough to step outside in faith, believing that God will stay right by his side.

And that's what I've got to do now. It's no good asking God to make me brave and then hiding away and avoiding what I'm scared of. I've got to step out in faith too.

I believe God will answer my prayers about other people. That's the faith Josh saw when we were running round the park and I asked him to pray for Mum. Now I've got to believe He'll answer when I pray about me. Every time you step out in faith, you get a bit stronger, Greg says. That's how faith grows. That's how I'll start being able to move my own mountains.

Greg is ace-in-your-face. The BPT wouldn't be the same without him.

Lord God, I want to be a house – with proper foundations and strong, straight walls. I'm stepping out in faith tomorrow. Please step with me. Amen.

AM

I went into the kitchen. Mum was wiping down the windowsill. There wasn't a yoghurt pot in sight.

I asked, 'What happened to Dad's beans?'

Mum said, 'Nothing. Not one, greeny-weeny, shooty-wooty thing. That's why they're in the bin.'

'Mum,' I said, 'you know my football boots?'

'You mean the ones that needed to go to the charity shop?' she said.

'That's them,' I said. 'Well, I was just wondering whether they actually ended up making it to the charity shop or whether, in fact, they might sort of … still … somehow … be … here.'

Mum stopped her wiping.

'Now, let me think,' she said. 'D'you know, I reckon they still might be.'

I said, 'Great. Only I think I might be going to need them today.'

She said, 'Now, why doesn't that surprise me?'

I thought for a minute, then, 'Mum,' I said. 'Why didn't you give them away?'

'Because,' she said, 'trying to imagine you not playing football is like trying to imagine Father Christmas without a beard.'

PM

After lunch Benny said, 'So, what's your creepy-crawly?'

I said, 'I've got no idea. To be honest, I've been a bit too busy to think about creepy-crawlies.'

'Busy doing what?' said Benny.

'Praying for one thing,' I said. 'In fact, that's pretty much it. I've been doing lots of praying.'

'Well,' said Josie, 'I think that can only be a good thing.'

'Thanks,' I said. 'Unfortunately, it's what Mr Mallory thinks that matters. I'm supposed to have a load of creepy-crawly project done by Friday. With pictures and everything.'

'Can't you think of something that's a bit like you?' Benny suggested. 'You know, like I did with a stick insect.'

'Not everyone thinks they're like an insect, though, Benny,' said Josie sensibly.

'I know!' squeaked Sarah. 'Maybe you'd find it easier to choose one if you could <u>imagine</u> yourself actually being a particular creepy-crawly. Like, say, a ladybird.'

'I don't think so,' I said.

'Why not?' she said.

'Because,' I said, 'I can't really imagine myself being small and red and covered in spots.'

Hid in the toilets after school. I haven't done that for ages. In fact I think the last time was in Year 2 when the juice bottle in my bag leaked all over my brand-new reading book. I was so scared of getting into trouble, I refused to come out even for the Head Teacher. In the end she had to phone Mum and ask her to come into school to have a word with me.

Mum did.

She said, 'Danny. Out. Now.'

I said, 'No, my reading book's all covered in juice.'

She said, '<u>You'll</u> be covered in juice if you don't come out.'

When I opened the door she gave me a huge cuddle and I think that might have been the first time she called me a wombat.

Yup, hiding in the toilets is always a dead giveaway that something pretty majorly serious is up – as John must have realised when he knocked on the cubicle door.

It went like this:

John: Danny, is that you?

Me: Why do you want to know?

John: Because if it is you, I was wondering if you were OK.

Me: Oh. And what if it isn't?

John: What if it isn't what?

Me: Me.

John: I haven't really thought about that because basically I know it's you.

Me: Oh.

John: So the thing is, why are you hiding in the toilets?

Me: Because I want to be a house. But if I'm going to be a house, I've got to be brave enough to start playing football again. Which isn't as easy as it sounds when you're scared of playing like a dork and having people make all sorts of unhelpful, dorky comments like, 'That's the goal over there – the thing with the posts.'

Only, I'm stepping out in faith today because I've asked God to be with me from the minute I put on my boots right through to when I take them off again after Mr Richardson's football club thingy. So however it goes it'll be OK because I won't be facing it on my own. Will I?

John: Sounds about right to me. But even if God is with you, you can't play football in the toilet, can you?

Me: Not really. Not enough leg room. You might get away with a bit of keepy-uppy, but that's about it.

John: So … are you coming out, then?

Me: I want to. I really do. It's just that I told you all I was never going to play football ever again, so if I do, you're all going to think I'm a nerd.

John: No, we're not. No one believed you anyway. By the way, why do you want to be a house?

***

Mr Richardson's after-school football club was totally ace-in-your face! There's one thing about stopping doing the thing you're craziest about in the whole universe – when you start doing it again, it's unbelievably off the planet!

I ran out onto the field hoping I could hide away somehow so nobody could see it was me. Which is actually pretty dumb when you come to think about it, because where can you hide on a football field? Mr Richardson spotted me straight away. In fact everyone spotted me straight away.

Mr Richardson said, 'Danny, my main trolley man. Glad you could make it.'

Benny said, 'Yeah! Stonking!'

Dave said, 'Wicked! Now you can help me with my dribbling.'

And Paul said, 'Are my shorts on the wrong way round?'

Cool. Ultra cool, actually. There's nothing like things getting back to how they were for helping you to feel … well … how you used to.

Afterwards, Paul said, 'You and football, you go together like me and computers. Nothing can come between me and my computer.'

'Or me and food,' grinned Benny.

'Or me and my bike,' added Dave.

That reminded me of Josh's favourite Bible verse.

'Or us and God's love,' I grinned. 'I've been talking to God a lot lately. And He's been talking to me. And brick by brick, He's going to build me into a house.'

'That's it!' shrieked Benny, suddenly beginning to flap his arms so excitedly, I wondered if he might take off. 'I've just thought of the PERFECT creepy-crawly for you.'

'What's that, then?' I asked.

'A praying mantis!'

Thank YOU for making me the PERFECT creepy-crawly! Amen.

Collect the set:

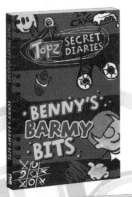

Christians needn't be boring
Benny's Barmy Bits
ISBN: 978-1-85345-431-8

You can always talk to God
Dave's Dizzy Doodles
ISBN: 978-1-85345-552-0

The Holy Spirit helps us live for Jesus
Gruff and Saucy's Topzy-Turvy Tales
ISBN: 978-1-85345-553-7

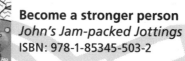

Become a stronger person
John's Jam-packed Jottings
ISBN: 978-1-85345-503-2

You can show God's love to others
Josie's Jazzy Journal
ISBN: 978-1-85345-457-8

Keep your friendships strong
Paul's Potty Pages
ISBN: 978-1-85345-456-1

You are special to God
Sarah's Secret Scribblings
ISBN: 978-1-85345-432-5

IF YOU LIKED THIS BOOK, YOU'LL LOVE THESE:

TOPZ

An exciting, day-by-day look at the Bible for children aged from 7 to 11. As well as simple prayers and Bible readings every day, each issue includes word games, puzzles, cartoons and contributions from readers. Fun and colourful, *Topz* helps children get to know God.
ISSN: 0967-1307
£2.75 each (bimonthly)
£14.95 UK annual subscription (six issues)
Prices shown are correct at time of printing.

TOPZ FOR NEW CHRISTIANS

Thirty days of Bible notes to help 7- to 11-year-olds find faith in Jesus and have fun exploring their new life with Him.
ISBN: 978-1-85345-104-1

TOPZ GUIDE TO THE BIBLE

A guide offering exciting and stimulating ways for 7- to 11-year-olds to become familiar with God's Word. With a blend of colourful illustrations, cartoons and lively writing, this is the perfect way to encourage children to get to know their Bibles.
ISBN: 978-1-85345-313-7

For current prices visit www.cwr.org.uk

National Distributors

UK: (and countries not listed below)
CWR, Waverley Abbey House, Waverley Lane, Farnham, Surrey GU9 8EP.
Tel: (01252) 784700 Outside UK (44) 1252 784700 Email: mail@cwr.org.uk

AUSTRALIA: KI Entertainment, Unit 21 317-321 Woodpark Road, Smithfield,
New South Wales 2164. Tel: 1 800 850 777 Fax: 02 9604 3699
Email: sales@kientertainment.com.au

CANADA: David C Cook Distribution Canada, PO Box 98,
55 Woodslee Avenue, Paris, Ontario N3L 3E5. Tel: 1800 263 2664
Email: swansons@cook.ca

GHANA: Challenge Enterprises of Ghana, PO Box 5723, Accra.
Tel: (021) 222437/223249 Fax: (021) 226227 Email: ceg@africaonline.com.gh

HONG KONG: Cross Communications Ltd, 1/F, 562A Nathan Road, Kowloon.
Tel: 2780 1188 Fax: 2770 6229 Email: cross@crosshk.com

INDIA: Crystal Communications, 10-3-18/4/1, East Marredpalli,
Secunderabad – 500026, Andhra Pradesh. Tel/Fax: (040) 27737145
Email: crystal_edwj@rediffmail.com

KENYA: Keswick Books and Gifts Ltd, PO Box 10242-00400, Nairobi.
Tel: (254) 20 312639/3870125 Email: keswick@swiftkenya.com

MALAYSIA: Canaanland, No. 25 Jalan PJU 1A/41B, NZX Commercial Centre,
Ara Jaya, 47301 Petaling Jaya, Selangor. Tel: (03) 7885 0540/1/2
Fax: (03) 7885 0545 Email: info@canaanland.com.my
Salvation Book Centre (M) Sdn Bhd, 23 Jalan SS 2/64, 47300 Petaling Jaya,
Selangor. Tel: (03) 78766411/78766797 Fax: (03) 78757066/78756360
Email: info@salvationbookcentre.com

NEW ZEALAND: KI Entertainment, Unit 21 317-321 Woodpark Road,
Smithfield, New South Wales 2164, Australia. Tel: 0 800 850 777
Fax: +612 9604 3699 Email: sales@kientertainment.com.au

NIGERIA: FBFM, Helen Baugh House, 96 St Finbarr's College Road, Akoka,
Lagos. Tel: (01) 7747429/4700218/825775/827264 Email: fbfm@hyperia.com

PHILIPPINES: OMF Literature Inc, 776 Boni Avenue, Mandaluyong City.
Tel: (02) 531 2183 Fax: (02) 531 1960 Email: gloadlaon@omflit.com

SINGAPORE: Alby Commercial Enterprises Pte Ltd, 95 Kallang Avenue #04-00,
AIS Industrial Building, 339420.Tel: (65) 629 27238 Fax: (65) 629 27235
Email: marketing@alby.com.sg

SOUTH AFRICA: Struik Christian Books, 80 MacKenzie Street, PO Box 1144,
Cape Town 8000. Tel: (021) 462 4360 Fax: (021) 461 3612
Email: info@struikchristianmedia.co.za

SRI LANKA: Christombu Publications (Pvt) Ltd, Bartleet House,
65 Braybrooke Place, Colombo 2. Tel: (9411) 2421073/2447665
Email: dhanad@bartleet.com

USA: David C Cook Distribution Canada, PO Box 98, 55 Woodslee Avenue,
Paris, Ontario N3L 3E5, Canada. Tel: 1800 263 2664 Email: swansons@cook.ca

CWR is a Registered Charity – Number 294387

CWR is a Limited Company registered in England – Registration Number
1990308